MW01234137

Victoria's Quest

Nancy Hagen
Patchen

Writer Works
West Lafayette, Indiana

©2004 Nancy Hagen Patchen
ISBN 0-9744415-0-3

Writers Works
1133 Glenway Street
West Lafayette, IN 47906

Book Design & Production
by
Whitney Scott

With love to Marty

With thanks
to the Women's Creative Writing Group

In cherished memory of Betsy Brewer

Such she often felt herself— struggling against terrific odds to maintain her courage; to say: 'But this is what I see; this is what I see,' and so to clasp some miserable remnant of her vision to her breast, which a thousand forces did their best to pluck from her.

—*To The Lighthouse,* Virginia Woolf

Being the Personal Log of
Victoria Willoughby of Chicago, Illinois

Entry 1 -- 13 Feb. 1868 – Weather: Brief sunshine in the a.m.

Dear Joseph,

It's mid-afternoon, not long before the early evening meal, and the light for writing is already fading. I smell steamy potatoes and cauliflower, boiling like a witches' brew, and some kind of fish half a day from rotten. I'll force down some bites for the sake of my health.

At least I have a room of my own where I can tend to heartsickness in solitude like an injured beast in a cave. Some of the women share space in larger rooms. A few minutes ago, down the hall from my closed door, a silly sounding voice called, "Please sit with me at the lunch table, dear Emma," and a second voice answered playfully, "Oh, that would be charming, Sarah." I shuddered and wrapped my purple shawl more tightly around my shoulders. I can't bear conversing with another human being at this time, trying to pass for normal when any moment I may go mad.

Yesterday I did manage to write and post that letter. Afterwards, on a secret walk, I sidled along the icy sidewalk and into a stationer's to buy this gray-covered book. It's half the size of the keeper's log. Its pages, unlined and white as snow, take on the first scratching of my pen like black paint on a fresh canvas. My desperate hope is that writing this account will hold my mind together until April. I feel invisible eyes watch – from the past, from the future? – as I sit on the hard chair at the high-legged table near the window. It's new, this writing. I have recorded little but for the lighthouse log, preferring to capture my world in images not words. The fairy tale books of my childhood I loved much more for the pictures than the stories.

So how did I come to be in this room with a crucifix above the bed and a view out the window of the sooty building next door? That's the story I want to tell. Perhaps it will be of interest to someone who sees my paintings, if they survive. There may be satisfaction, too, in the telling, some reliving of contentment and joy. Filling this page, now turning to the top of the next, lifts my courage – like mixing my paints on a palette and washing my brushes before daring to dash on the first stroke of paint.

My hands are trembling. The bracelet on my wrist clicks on the table top. This silver bracelet that I wear every day. Yes, that's the first story to tell, my memory of first wearing it that hot summer day when I was five.

The Bracelet
(Shoreside Light, Indiana, August 1851)

I was jarred out of a dream by Mama's singing below me in the kitchen. Her high sweet voice lilted a gay song amid the clatter of dishes and her quick step between stove and table. That was a good sign, her singing, and I remembered we were going over to Shoreside today. In my bed, I stretched and wiggled my toes, glad to shake off a bad dream. Listening to Mama sing, I watched light from the small high window spill into the room. It was early but my bedroom was growing warm.

Above me in the lighthouse tower the floor boards creaked and Papa clumped around, thump, THUMP, thump, THUMP, taking down and cleaning the lanterns that had burned through the night. Quickly, I got up and pulled on the green cotton dress I wore when we went off the island among other people. Just ahead of me, Papa limped down the black spiral staircase to the kitchen. He was dressed in his old blue ship captain uniform with a double row of gold buttons down the front and a matching blue cap.

Mama stopped her song and smiled. "If it isn't Captain Willoughby. How handsome you look, Sir." She poured coffee into Papa's mug as he sat down at the table.

"Not much to being captain of this ship," he said, holding his back straight.

Mama's soft blue dress matched the melting blue of her eyes. Her red hair was pulled up high and fastened with a comb. She stood me by the window and quickly braided my hair and buttoned the back of my dress. "Now, sit with Papa, Victoria. We'll eat and be on our way," she said.

She set bowls of hot oatmeal at our places. The silver bracelet that Papa had given her tinkled when her wrist bumped the bowls.

"Oh, Mama, could I wear your bracelet today?" I begged.

Mama laughed and said, "Oh, why not," ignoring Papa's dark look. She undid the clasp and wrapped it twice around my wrist. I brushed a finger over the delicate silver links of stars and ovals, moving my hand for the light to catch the purple stones that filled the ovals and twinkled in the center of the stars. Papa had bought it from a foreign sailor and said it was probably from India.

After breakfast, Mama washed the dishes and I dried them while Papa drank a second cup of coffee. Before we went out the door, Mama put some letters in her string shopping bag. I had nothing to carry but I felt important wearing the bracelet.

Outside, the sun burned amid a cushion of white clouds. The American flag gently flapped at the top of the pole near the front door. We made our way down the little hill to the wooden boathouse where Papa kept the rowboats. Inside, the odor of seaweed hung over the gently rocking boats.

"Watch out for the alligator," Papa said.

I stepped away, frowning at the shadowy water where a pair of bulbous eyes and a leathery back might surface.

"Victoria, Papa's teasing," Mama said as he gave her a steadying hand to step into the boat and lifted me onto the little wooden seat in the middle. He untied the rope, climbed in, and we drifted out onto the lake. Papa began to dip the oars in and out of the water in a rhythm as smooth as the chords Mama played on the piano. Sitting backwards in front of him, I watched the lighthouse slowly shrink to the size of a toy. Two hours felt like a day to travel the three miles across Lake Michigan from the island to town. I trailed my hand in the water, cold even in high summer. Mama sat at the opposite end from Papa, looking past both of us at the approaching town. Her eyes sparkled from reflected sunlight on the waves.

Before I was born, Papa had built a small private dock on shore so he didn't have to go all the way into Shoreside Harbor. Once we arrived and the boat was tied up, Mama and I disappeared into a clump of scrub pines to relieve ourselves. Then I ran up the sandy shore, giddy with the freedom of an open stretch of land, until Papa called me back. We crossed the beach and a wide swath of rough grass until we reached Front Street, the north end of Shoreside. We headed south through streets noisy with the sound of carriage wheels and clomping of horses' feet. Horses terrified me, their gigantic dark bodies and long slender legs ending in metal hooves. Every time we passed one, I closed my eyes and clung to Mama's skirt.

At the corner of Main and Front, Papa left us. We would meet at the boat when the clock on St. Catherine's Catholic Church struck two. That would give Papa time to get home and ready the night lanterns. He was going to the bank and then stopping to see his Cousin Sherman, who owned an important business in town. Mama and I went to Strachey's

Victoria's Quest

General Store to order groceries and ask for mail. Mr. Strachey was the postmaster, too. The store smelled strongly of freshly ground coffee beans and spicy pickles that floated in a briny barrel near the counter. While Mama bought the usual – pork, bacon, potatoes, cheese, apples, oatmeal, flour and butter – I sucked the peppermint stick Mr. Strachey, who was short and round, plucked from a tall glass jar next to the cash drawer. I crunched the last slivers on the way to Depot Street where Mama's friends Maggie and Frank Fogarty lived. They were not related to us like Cousin Sherman and his wife Abigail, but I called them Aunt and Uncle. Their house was across from the small railroad station. The tracks ran through the middle of the street. Mama said mill and factory workers lived in the row houses. Uncle Frank worked in the lumber mill. The houses looked the same except for the colors of the front doors. The Fogartys' door was yellow.

Maggie filled the frame of the door when she opened it. She was as big as Mama was small and slender. She scooped both of us into her large, warm arms. "Oh, Kathleen, it's so grand to see you. And Victoria, oh for sure you're a little thing like your mother. Come in, come in!"

Mama looked at Aunt Maggie's stomach, which seemed very round. "So there will soon be another Fogarty?"

Aunt Maggie sighed. "Yes, God's will is for there to be another mouth to feed at our table." She turned and called. "Children, come play with Victoria!"

Patricia and Bridget, both older than me, arrived to take me confidently by the hand while Peter, who was my age, trailed behind the three of us. Aunt Maggie led everyone to the kitchen. "My newest quilt, Kathleen," she said, "but I wish I had prettier patterns to use." She pushed a large square of cloth made of sewn smaller pieces to a corner of the table to make room for the cups of cool water she poured. "It looks very nice, Maggie," Mama protested. "You are a wonder with a needle." After we had finished drinking, Aunt Maggie shooed us into the back yard, saying, "We want to talk about the old days, when WE were girls." She and Mama laughed.

I was unused to other children but the Fogartys didn't seem to notice. We played hopscotch and then tag until we were out of breath and threw ourselves on the ground, fanning each other and laughing. Then Mama called, "Victoria, it's time to go. Come in and show Aunt Maggie the bracelet." I looked down and saw my wrist was bare.

When I told Mama, she cried, "Oh, no!" and ran out to look all over the ground. Then we went back in and searched every inch of the house.

"I'm sorry, Mama, I'm sorry," I said over and over.

She wrung her hands and paced and repeated, "Edward is going to kill me." Maggie crossed herself and looked up to the ceiling.

When we had to give up on the bracelet being somewhere at the Fogartys, we retraced our steps through town, collecting the packages at Strachey's and asking everyone we saw if they'd seen it. Every head shook no. Finally, we went back to the boat to wait for Papa. Mama leaned into the boat to search the bottom and poked among the pebbles at the edge of the shore. I followed my morning footprints up the beach, poking a stick among the broken shells and strands of seaweed. Miraculously, I spotted a silver glint in the sand and picked up the bracelet. Sobbing, I brought it to Mama. She brushed off the sand and put it on her wrist. "You'll never wear this again as long as I live," she vowed. But in this prediction as in many other things, Mama was wrong.

Entry 2 -- 14 Feb. 1868 – Weather: Slight thaw; lake ice cracking

Dear Joseph,

At odd moments, day or night, I hear Mama's piano crackle like heat lightning. A violent dance music of reckless polkas. It's in my head, of course. Musical instruments are not allowed here. We are supposed to reflect in silence on our sins and the worldly pleasures we have indulged in too freely. Mama is not here, either, though she lives elsewhere in this big city. We are like fog-blind ships on Lake Michigan. At this moment, is she playing the piano in O'Keefe's while I once again ponder the mystery and pain of being her daughter? I grant she did give me an artistic sensibility. Indeed, I have her piano playing to thank for my existence. A year or so after the day of the almost-lost bracelet, the first Mama, as I think of her, enchanted me with the tale of meeting Papa because of the piano. All children love to hear how their parents met with the inevitably satisfying result of their birth. A pity I won't be able to tell such a story to my daughter when she is six years old...

Over and over, I've pictured this encounter in the Tavistock, Papa with his dark beard and whiskery sideburns, Mama with her rich golden red hair, he of few words charmed by her easy talk and careless laughter. She must have seen the darkness hovering around him, this darkness I also know, while he was drawn to her as a lantern that chases away shadows. Now, as I record the story she told me, I know her lantern had already lost its glow and his darkness was well settled in around the three of us.

The Piano
(Shoreside Light, October 1852)

It was a rainy fall day and I was helping Mama dust the parlor. The air was damp and the fire sputtered and crackled around the logs in the fireplace. I rubbed a cloth across the piano top, looking out the window

Victoria's Quest

at the gray wetness. My hand slipped and hit two keys, causing a thunderous rumble and me to jump. Mama laughed and straightened up from polishing the table next to Papa's chair. She came over to the piano and ran her fingers smoothly up the keyboard, one hand crossing swiftly over the other, until she plinked the last white key, the highest note.

"Did you know, Victoria, the piano was our matchmaker – Papa's and mine?" she asked gaily.

"What's a matchmaker?" This sounded scary to me, like something to do with fire, the fire we must always be careful to have only in the lanterns and the fireplace.

"Something that brings two people together." She sat on the narrow piano bench and played a few brisk chords.

"This piano did that?" I asked when she stopped, the music still echoing around us.

"No, no, the piano at the Tavistock tavern in Shoreside."

"How old were you?" I wiggled myself up on the bench next to her, excited at the start of a story.

"Only seventeen." Mama patted my hand. "I was a maid for the rich lumber mill owner, Mr. Nicolson. Your Aunt Maggie was, too. We lived in."

"What do maids do?" I wondered.

"What you and I are doing right now." Mama rolled her eyes.

"And how old was Papa?"

"About thirty."

"That sounds old."

"I guess it would to you," Mama agreed. "But Papa had already been a ship captain for a few years."

"How did he know you were at Mr. Nicolson's?" I wanted her to tell the story faster.

"Well, he didn't. He docked one night in Shoreside on his way to New York and came in the Tavistock to visit Cousin Sherman. I was upstairs in the dance hall playing the piano."

"Was that part of being a maid?"

Mama laughed. "Aunt Maggie and I got Saturday night off sometimes and when we did we went dancing at the Tavistock. There was an old piano up there and the fiddle player showed me some chords so I could play along with him. Here, this is one of the reels your Aunt Maggie and Uncle Frank loved. They met in the dance hall, too." Her fingers bounced over the keys while I clapped my hands to the rhythm. Mama's face always lit up when she played.

16

When she stopped, she sat quietly watching raindrops dribble down the window. "Papa told me later he was going to leave until he heard overhead music and the thumping of feet. He followed the sound upstairs to the dance hall."

"Does Papa dance?" I asked, amazed at the idea and swinging my legs back and forth under the bench.

Mama sighed. "No, he doesn't, but he likes to listen to music. And when he walked in, he was so handsome in that smart uniform, so different from the farmers and mill workers, I stopped in the middle of a chord. He marched straight across the room to the piano and said, 'Miss, please keep playing' like it was an order. He gave me his name and inquired mine."

"'Kathleen Flinn, if you please, Captain Edward Willoughby. Have you sailed to the edge of the world and caught a sea monster?' I replied."

"'No, Miss Flinn,' he answered, shaking his head. 'I've only sailed up and down the Great Lakes.'"

Mama smiled. "Then he asked if I cared to take a break from playing the piano and take a walk to the harbor. I said I wouldn't mind. Maggie and Frank came with us. He pointed out his ship."

"What was it like?"

"Big and handsome like Papa." Mama smoothed her skirt.

"Then what happened?" I asked.

"He offered me a different life and I wanted that," Mama murmured.

I didn't understand this. "Didn't he have to go back to his ship?"

Mama's voice went high. "Yes, but he docked twice more in Shoreside that year and came to see me at Mr. Nicolson's. Then in a storm on the following voyage, he had his accident, the falling beam that crushed his leg. That sealed the match."

"Fire?" I asked, lost again.

Mama frowned. "What I mean is Papa's sailing days were over. With his connections, Cousin Sherman arranged for him to be appointed to care for the lighthouse. The present keeper had gotten too old for the work. Papa said if I'd marry him, he'd buy me a piano."

"You said 'yes.'" I hugged myself.

"I did," Mama said in a faraway voice. "We went off and got married by a judge with his wife and clerk as our witnesses. It was so romantic, running off to a lighthouse on an island with a handsome sea captain, especially one who put a fine spinet for me in the parlor. The first year..."

Abruptly, Mama stopped talking.

I looked up and saw Papa lumbering up the hill toward us from the boathouse. Even from here, I could see his frown.

"Tell me more, Mama," I begged.

"I have to start supper." She got up and left the room, leaving me looking at the silent piano keys.

That night, as I was going up to bed, Papa ordered me as usual to say my prayers. Then Mama kissed me, cloaking me in her scent of lilac. Close to her, I smelled something else, a harsher scent, sweet but not like flowers and so strong I coughed.

After she left, I frowned, pulled the covers around me, and stared long into the darkness before sleep came. Sometime later, I awakened to an odd whirring sound, not in my room but somewhere above in the lighthouse. Trembling yet wild with curiosity, I got out of bed and opened the door. Below me, darkness. Above, a flutter of whiteness, a moan, neither human nor animal. A ghost?

"Hello," I quavered, the word echoing up the stairwell like a sparrow's wings. "Go to sleep, Victoria," came Papa's voice from the tower.

I backed into my room, swung the door shut, and pushed the dollhouse against it. I sat on the bed, waiting and crying in my fear, but nothing happened. At last, I crawled under the covers again and fell asleep, dried tears on my cheeks.

Entry 3 -- 15 Feb. 1868 – Weather: Sharp winds, snow

Dear Joseph,

My heart pounded when I heard Sister Margaret call out "Inspection" and rap on my door this morning. I've only been here two days and had forgotten our rooms are checked on Saturday mornings before visiting hours. My mind scrabbled like a frantic mouse until I remembered where I'd hidden this log. (You recall my telling you I spent years doing the same with my pencil sketches to avoid trouble.) I'd been shoving it under the mattress, which was tiring, and had just shifted it under my undergarments in the small dresser.

After she left, I laid on the bed an hour, recovering from the intrusion. Like spoiled cream in a jug, her sourness seemed to linger in the air along with the actual smell of her stale clothing. I heard one of the girls say the nuns are not eager to have their habits washed. The heavy material takes a week to dry in winter.

Anyway, Sister Margaret didn't wear white gloves like Mr. Mackelhorn, the lighthouse inspector, but her frown was as disapproving and her manner as skeptical. Despite her bulky habit, she stepped briskly on her rounds, eyeing the cleanliness of the washbowl and neatness of the bedclothes and asking short, unfriendly questions of my bodily functions. She frowned at the window, seemingly affronted by the wind rattling and the snowflakes clinging to the glass. Except for the thick rimless glasses behind which her eyes shone like blue marbles, how indeed she reminded me of Mr. Mackelhorn. On his quarterly visits, he marched like a soldier around the island and in and out of the lighthouse asking Papa sharp questions about how he was taking care of the property and lanterns, keeping the log, and using the funds of the Lighthouse Board in Detroit.

I noticed today Sister Margaret's face and hands were the yellow-white of candle wax. That's all the skin I can see of hers or any of the nuns. Swaddling clothes – swaddling oneself for God – no flesh to tempt or be tempted. I wonder what her body is like unclothed – worthy of a nude painting? (She'd no doubt be shocked at my speculations. She doesn't yet know I'm an artist. I've kept that to myself for now.)

I'm not sure if I'm imagining that Sister Margaret doesn't like me in particular. When I told Mother Superior my mother was Irish, she said Sister Margaret was, too, from County Cork. Maybe I can say something to her about what we have in common.

As far as visitors go, I came here to avoid anyone I know in Chicago or Shoreside finding me. I will be glad to stay in my room while the other women – girls, we're called – see the friends or family who risk coming into our shameful presence.

Later... After lunch, I slept a little, the words inspection, visitors, washing clothes somehow repeating. When I awoke to the sound of voices in the hall, another childhood memory hovered around me, awaiting recall, something to do with someone's clothes drying, a visitor. Oh, yes, oh, yes, the unexpected visitor to the lighthouse who changed our lives. How old was I? Seven, I think. I'll write it down before it's time for supper.

Visitor
(Shoreside Light, June 1853)

My earliest memory of Mama playing the piano was for Mr. Mackelhorn after he finished lunch. "You certainly have a fine piano there, Mrs. Willoughby," he'd say, as he laid down his fork.

That was Mama's cue. "Would you care to hear a few tunes before you set sail, Mr. Mackelhorn?"

He'd sit on the sofa, drinking coffee, tapping his foot, and watching Mama. A few feet away Papa settled in his easy chair, also watching Mama, and I sat on the floor, playing with my dollhouse.

Papa was never sure which day Mr. Mackelhorn would arrive in the official round-hulled boat that brought quarterly supplies of kerosene and other necessities. When we saw it in the distance, we scurried around like chickens with their heads cut off trying to get the lighthouse and island in perfect order before he set foot on it.

Even so, Mr. Mackelhorn's were the only regular visits of any kind, the others being only a fisherman or sailor Papa hauled in on a stormy night.

One early summer night, the sound of boots stomping in the kitchen below woke me. Papa's cold voice said, "There's the stove to sit by," followed by Mama's quick, "First, take off those wet things and wrap yourself in this blanket," and then a gasp, "Why, Dennis Flanagan, as I live and breathe. What happened?"

The man's voice sounded weak compared to Papa's. "I was out fishing like a fool and my boat hit the shoals. Kathleen Flinn, is it? I forgot you were out here. Aren't you a sight for sore eyes tonight?"

Mama laughed. "Why, thank you kindly." The coffeepot rattled on the stove. I heard the sound every morning. "I think you need a bit of whiskey in your cup, Dennis," she said.

"In here, Flanagan," Papa called from the parlor.

"Thank you, Sir," the man said, and I fell back to sleep.

In the morning, Mr. Flanagan, still wrapped in a blanket, ate breakfast and talked. His clothes, hanging to dry above the stove, filled the kitchen with the smell of wool. His family and Mama's, it turned out, lived on neighboring farms outside Shoreside. He had sandy-colored hair and green eyes I couldn't stop staring at as I silently ate my oatmeal across the kitchen table. He and Mama talked about growing up and riding horses when they were children.

"I'm afraid I've lost her," he said. It took me a moment to realize he meant his boat. I wondered why he didn't sound more unhappy about it, but then he didn't depend on fishing for a living. He smiled and told Mama about the farm families she knew – the Donnegans, who'd bought more acres and were working themselves to death to feed their seven children; the Millers, who came into some money from a rich relative they never knew in Chicago but didn't seem to spend any of it, on anything a body could see, anyway, not going into town anymore than they ever did; and his own family, the Flanagans, who were doing all right, but Dennis himself was itching to do something with his life.

Mama spooned more eggs onto his plate and said, "Like what, Dennis?"

He looked up at her. "Chicago sounds mighty interesting to me," he said. "It's growing fast, with all sorts of work for able-bodied men. I'd like to see what big city life is like."

21

Mama turned her back and put the skillet on the stove. "Yes, that would be exciting."

Papa set down his coffee cup. "Lots of trouble is what it's like, nobody God fearing, people always out to cheat you, and the place is built on a swamp."

Mr. Flanagan laughed and stood up. He wasn't nearly as tall as Papa. "I can take care of myself."

Mama sent me outside to play for a while. Ever since I could walk, she had tied a rope around my waist with the other end attached to the flagpole so I couldn't wander off and fall in the water. This morning she forgot, and I was pleased. I was too big to be put on the rope. To prove it, I stayed around the lighthouse until she called. When I came in the kitchen, she was reaching above the stove to touch Mr. Flanagan's shirt and trousers. "A little damp, but wearable," she announced.

"Yes," Papa said, "If you want to be rowed to town, it's time to go."

Mr. Flanagan dressed upstairs in Mama and Papa's bedroom while Mama sat down at the piano and played a loud tune. As she finished, he clattered down the stairs, exclaiming, "That was wonderful, Kathleen! It's such a treat to hear your music again. You should have an audience who pays to hear you."

Mama laughed. "Perhaps we'll see you more often when we come into town this summer."

But when he said he went dancing every Saturday at the Tavistock, she looked away.

He pulled a penny out of his pocket and handed it to me. "Here, you're a pretty lass. Don't think I didn't notice you." He caught my eye and winked.

I blushed and whispered a thank you, looking at the floor next to the piano. Mama quickly rose from the bench and offered her hand. "Best you don't go fishing for a while now." She and Mr. Flanagan laughed, their hands clasped.

Papa limped to the front door, opened it, and waited for our visitor. "Last chance to go," he said, as if Mr. Flanagan were a sailor who had failed several times at some task and the captain had run out of patience.

That night Mama played the piano for hours and when she kissed me goodnight, I again inhaled that sweet, harsh smell mixed in with her lilac perfume.

Entry 4 -- 17 Feb. 1868 -- Weather: Blizzard

Dear Joseph,

Late this morning I opened the front door after Sister Rosamund's sewing class to an angry vortex of snow and wind spiraling beneath a gray sky. In Chicago, February weather is as terrible as that of December. Lake Michigan is merciless to all who dare to live near it through the winter. I should have closed the door and returned to my room, but the last two days of harsh winter have been as endless as those of lighthouse winters and I was desperate to break the spell with some fresh air. Wrapping myself in every layer of clothing I had, I pushed out the door into the shock of the cold wind. Slowly, head bent and stomach knotted, I trudged east, then south, then west to circle the city block. Out of the corner of my eye, I glimpsed bright color in a shop window and pressed close. It turned out to be a hat shop and a quick memory of my old room at Mrs. Barlow's flashed before the falling curtain of white closed my view again. Suddenly, a helpless rage seized me about my life – art, Papa, Mama, the hidden I always want to make visible.

In that moment I became a child again, in a different snowstorm, running up to the lighthouse tower, straining at the window for a glimpse of Shoreside, breathing in the sweet biscuit scent that had followed me up the staircase. I pressed my hot face to the icy glass, trying to see a far-off building, any building, to feel a distance from the lighthouse. I couldn't make sense of why Papa had gotten so angry at me just now in the kitchen...

I slid and nearly fell on an icy patch of the Chicago sidewalk. It took a few minutes for my heart to slow and my blood to stop pulsing in my ears but I welcomed the surge of warmth to my body. I continued to hug myself through the stinging wind back to the home.

As I staggered in, dumb from cold, Sister Rosamund clomped out of the parlor in her long-gaited way. With her heavily lidded eyes, rounded lower face and protruding teeth, she reminds me of a bad-tempered camel.

Victoria's Quest

"What's this? A ghost?" She gasped at my snow-caked garments. "You're forbidden to go out alone, Victoria, and in this weather!"

"I'm sorry, Sister." I clenched my teeth to still their rattling. "I needed some fresh air."

"There is plenty of it if you open your window." Sister Rosamund sniffed and turned on her heel.

In my room, shuddering with chills, I pulled off boots and laid my soaked outer clothes across the sink. In my chemise I got into bed and curled in a ball under the heavy wool blanket, ignoring the lunch bell that rang a short time later. The blizzard wore on, howling at the window pane. When I finally warmed enough to get up again, I wrapped myself in the blanket and sat at my desk. Ever since I arrived at the home, memories of the past have stabbed me like ice picks any time of day or night and can be put to rest only when I write them in my log.

Hard Winter
(Shoreside Light, March 1854)

The year 1854 was one of the worst winters ever on Lake Michigan. Cold weather came early and there was storm after storm. Boat traffic ceased a month early. By late November, the lake was frozen in large patches of floating ice. In some places, close to shore, the ice froze solid, waves taken by surprise and frozen in mid-curl. There was no way of knowing how solid the ice was, so I could play no further than the shore of the island.

The winter drove us inside and farther apart. In January, the temperature hung below zero for ten days. Time crawled in a smothering darkness and chill. Often in the morning, ice formed crystal patterns on the inside of the lighthouse walls. I pretended I lived in a fairy tale winter palace to forget how long I had lain awake the night before, listening to the storm shriek around the lighthouse and below in the parlor Mama's angry questions of why there was never any money left from Papa's pay, why she couldn't buy nice things when they went to town, why she had to be marooned on the island, and Papa's answering silence as frightening as her shrill voice.

Besides routine chores, Mama had little to occupy her during the day. Papa spent a lot of time up in the tower even though there were no lanterns to light or keep clean and only weather to record in the log. Mama gave big sighs, her lips moving, as she worked around the house. Waiting for something to come out of the oven, she muttered and rocked at the kitchen table with her cup of tea. Sometimes I could cheer her up by asking for stories about her and Maggie at Mr. Ramsay's house and her life in town.

On weekdays, I spent the morning sitting at the kitchen table and working my way through pages of mail-order grammar, spelling, and math books with Papa's help. The island was too far for me to go to school in Shoreside, even when we weren't marooned by weather. Not that Papa could afford, on his keeper's salary, the tuition of the private academy Paul and Michael Willoughby, Cousin Sherman's sons, attended. "Everyone should know how to read, write, and do sums," Papa declared. "That's enough for girls."

Night after night, Mama played and sang songs at the piano, ten or twelve, the fingers of her left hand splayed in chords, her right hand picking out the tune. Sometimes, she stood up and curtsied after a song as if she were on stage. One night, she began to teach me a tune but Papa said, "One piano player is enough in this family," and I went back to my dollhouse.

His bad leg propped on a stool, Papa spent his evenings whittling animals from pieces of wood. He had already built the dollhouse, all the furniture, and a family of four, parents and their two children, a boy and a girl. Often he read the Bible his mother sent him before she died. He always called her "my poor mother..." The first time he said it, I asked if she lived in a shack and had enough to eat. He shook his head and said, "No, I mean poor in another way. Never mind." Once he showed me where she had written his name in the Bible, *Edward Trygve Willoughby, born Jan. 11, 1805.* His first and last name were English, but his middle name was Norwegian. Trig-vee was how you said it. He asked if I knew Norwegians were among the earliest peoples to have lighthouses. He said the Atlantic coast of Norway is lined with fingers of water surrounded by high mountains called fjords, which you said as fee-ords. Safe harbors were hard for sailors to see, so people kept bonfires burning on top of mountains so they could be seen from the ocean.

"I'm glad we have lights instead of fire for ships to see." I closed my book of fairy tales.

"We still have to be careful with fire, Victoria," he said. "Now up to bed and say your prayers." That night, Mama smelled only of lilac.

One bitter dark March morning, as another snowstorm howled around the lighthouse, I could barely stay awake. Looking up, I saw a pattern of ice on the kitchen window that looked like a man. A man with horns for ears. I tore out a piece of paper from my copy book when Mama had turned away to pull a pan of biscuits from the oven. I stared at the man on the window and moved my hand in imitation of the outline. The shed door outside the kitchen flew open. Papa stomped in with an armful of newly split wood. He glanced at my paper and quickly dumped the wood into the box by the stove. The next thing I knew, he had snatched it up and torn it to pieces.

I leapt up. "Papa!" I cried.

"You're giving form to Satan," he said, walking to the stove. "I won't have you drawing such blasphemy. It's unChristian." He yanked off the lid of the damper, stuffed in the paper, and dropped in a match. It felt like he had set me aflame as well as the drawing.

"Oh, for heaven's sake, Edward," Mama said, with a small smile toward me.

"Kathleen, you know what sin is, being a Catholic," Papa said, scowling.

Mama turned away, jabbing a fork under each biscuit and moving it onto a plate.

I ran from the kitchen and up the stairs to the tower window. I stared at the blinding whiteness, wishing I could escape across the frozen lake, feeling something had been taken away from me, something that I didn't even know I had until a few minutes ago.

Entry 5 -- 27 Feb. 1868 -- Weather: Cold and dry

Dear Joseph,

Sister Margaret had some kind of stroke last week, I'm sure of it, now that I've seen her again today. We were told she had a mild fever, but stout Dr. Stephens called three times, puffing up the stairs with his black satchel. I meant to explain earlier that we girls live on the first floor and all the nuns on the second, ten in all. Three are in charge of us – Sister Margaret, Sister Rosamund, and Sister Barbara, the cook – while the other seven are out teaching at St. Mary's Primary School during the day. They room in twos except for Mother Superior, who has her own room. All the nuns are older than they look, I think, piety keeping faces unlined and habits covering the ravages of time that can not be overcome by prayer. Sister Margaret's roommate is Sister Winifred, who acts so timid I can't imagine her standing before a classroom. But maybe that's only the way she acts around Sister Margaret.

And how strangely things have changed between us this afternoon! A short time ago, chilled and nauseated, I went to the kitchen at the back of the house to make a cup of tea. It's Thursday when Sister Barbara goes to the fish market. Not that I was sneaking. Sister Barbara does not enforce the rule that the girls are not allowed kitchen privileges. She welcomes anyone coming in to chat, which gives her the chance to sit down and rest her arthritic legs. Alice is her most frequent visitor and even manages to compliment her meals. I don't know how, given the near inedibility of her concoctions, like the sausage, squash and cabbage stew, though I should be the last one to complain.

I walked in and lit the stove to heat a kettle of water. Then I turned to the cupboard to take out a cup, facing the kitchen table for the first time.

I jumped at the sight of Sister Margaret sitting at the far end, weeping. With her left hand she struggled to fit a pen into the lifeless fingers of her right hand. Like the desk of an impatient schoolgirl, the table before her was strewn with crumpled pieces of paper. I noticed also a bottle of ink, a sheaf of blank paper, and a letter addressed to her in large flowing script.

Victoria's Quest

"I keep a diary," I blurted, horrified by my words as soon as they escaped my mouth. I pulled a handkerchief from my sleeve and offered it. Sister Margaret shook her head and closed her eyes. Tears slid under the rim of her glasses like rain drops on a window pane.

"I'm making tea. Would you like a cup?" I asked.

"Sister Barbara shouldn't allow anyone to use her kitchen," she answered. Her words were a reflex for she didn't object when I poured tea in two cups, brought them to the table, and sat down. She tapped a blank piece of paper. "My brother's school is closed for repairs and he's visiting family in Ireland. I want to write him a letter." Awkwardly, she lifted the cup with her left hand and sipped the tea.

"He's a teacher?"

"At a Catholic boys' school on the South Side. Dennis is a Brother, and I'm a Sister," she said without humor.

"Your family must be proud," I said quickly, startled by the name Dennis. Feverishly, I searched my memory for Sister Margaret's last name. Surely not Flanagan, and, if so, surely not the same man I had known. I could see no resemblance in her face.

"Yes," she said shortly. "I want to write him a letter," she repeated, "but this hand..." She broke off, nearly dropping her cup.

"You could dictate a letter to me."

"He knows my handwriting. I don't want him to know I've had a ... I'm not my usual self."

"I think no letter at all from his sister would worry him more than a letter in handwriting he's not used to," I dared to say.

She stared at me. "I came to the kitchen so Sister Winifred wouldn't concern herself with my efforts." The old anger coated her voice. "I didn't think this task would be so impossible."

"Please. Let me help. I won't tell anyone." I spoke in a near whisper, wondering why I did so.

She lifted her eyebrows and shrugged.

There were long pauses as the nun composed her thoughts. She asked a number of questions of Dennis and news of the cousin's family with whom he was staying and said, as for her, life at the home was proceeding as usual. How little we say in letters. How much must be read between the lines. I wondered if Sister Margaret's brother would do so. She had me sign it with her Christian name only, Margaret, and then address it, to my great relief, to a Mr. Dennis Kelly.

The nun thanked me and smiled. I went straight back to my room to write in the log, my mind suddenly flooded with memories of the day I wrote another letter, one to Mama, never sent, and of the fire that followed.

Fire

(Shoreside Light, September 1856)

S itting cross-legged on the grass, I bent over a piece of paper, the pencil thick in my ten-year-old fingers. I'd been outside all afternoon in the warm brightness, soft breezes blowing, the lake glittering in the sun. There was not a hint that summer was over. Only now was the light beginning to fade.

> *Dear Mama,*
> *This afternoon I brought the dollhouse family*
> *outside to play. The dollhouse is too heavy*
> *to carry out here. It is very warm for*
> *late September. Indian summer, Papa says. I*
> *named the sister Virginia and the brother*
> *James. They are having a picnic.*

Where are you, Mama? I cried inwardly. *When are you coming back?* When I asked Papa those questions, he stared at me as if I were asking about the devil himself, or someone he'd never heard of. I was writing to Mama to convince myself she still existed. For weeks I had left food on my plate and started awake three or four times during the night, my heart skittering in my chest. Mama's presence was a ghost self. I saw her stooped in the vegetable garden to pull weeds, pinning our clothes on the line with Papa's shirts flying like sails, holding up her skirt and doing a little jig when the sun came out. Inside the lighthouse, her lilac scent lingered in every room... Yet I couldn't get my fingers to write the words *Mama, Please come home.*

It had been weeks since that pretty Saturday the three of us had rowed to town. We had lunch at Cousin Sherman's. Mama ate little and laughed shrilly at everything Cousin Sherman said. Cousin Abigail looked on with a thin smile. Mama said she would like to see the Fogartys before we left town. We could take our time and meet her at Strachey's. A little less than an hour later, Papa and I walked to the general store. With a curious look, the storekeeper handed Papa a letter. "Mrs. Willoughby left this for you." Papa left the store without me. "Here, choose whatever piece you like, Victoria," Mr. Strachey said hastily, lifting the lid off the candy jar. I plucked out one without looking, said thank you, and hurried outside. Papa was already stuffing the letter in his pocket.

"Time to go home," he said in the cold voice that frightened me.

"Aren't we going to wait for Mama?" My eyes darted up and down, willing Mama to come toward us, waving and smiling.

Papa took my arm and jerked me toward the beach. "She doesn't want to be found. We are going to get along by ourselves from now on."

As he rowed silently to the island and I sucked on the licorice, I remembered the faraway smile on Mama's face the past several days. How she had stopped playing the piano or having bad words with Papa or even telling me to do my chores.

That night, numb from crying that Papa pretended not to hear, I crawled into bed and then gasped at the sudden touch of Mama's silver bracelet under my pillow. Feverishly, I wrapped it around my wrist and hugged it to my heart until my flesh warmed its coldness. It was our secret, Mama's and mine. Mama did love me, she must, to give me her precious bracelet! But in the next moment, I was back to the thought that had stabbed me like a sharp shore rock all day. *Why had she left us, left me?* Gasping with fresh tears, I tore off the bracelet, scratching my wrist, and flung it away. Pounding a fist on the mattress, I pushed my head deep into the pillow to smother my sobs.

A drop of water fell on Mama's letter. Rain. I looked up and saw storm clouds, puffy and dark, moving toward the island. Wind ruffled the grass and whipped the flag. I saw Papa come out of the boathouse and peer at the sky, then trudge up the little hill toward me.

"Get inside before it storms. I'm going to get the lanterns up now. You'd best try to make some supper," he said, frowning at the paper in my lap.

I got up quickly and followed him across the stone steps and into the lighthouse. In the kitchen, I crumpled Mama's letter and burned it in the stove. *Why should I write to her if she didn't write to me?*

Thunder rolled, and through the yellow-curtained window the sky further darkened. And then, with a sudden tremendous crack, lightning struck the lighthouse. Above me, I heard Papa's voice calling. I ran from the kitchen and tumbled up the circle of dark steps. When I reached the second floor, where the two bedrooms were, I heard Papa's hoarse "Fire!"

Bumping my ankles into the hard step edges, I rushed to the next level and yanked open the door. Across the room where gray dusk hung at the windows, Papa lay sprawled at the foot of the tower ladder, staring at his right arm. Nearby, fire shot up from a broken lantern on the floor. "Lightning," he rasped, jerking his head. I understood at once. The last bolt of lightning had struck him as he grasped the iron ladder to climb up to the Fresnel lens.

Papa dropped his head again. The lantern fire took off, gobbling up kerosene that spilled in a thick black arc across the floor to Papa's desk. On the back of his chair, I spied the brown wool shawl he wore in cold weather. I snatched it up, threw it over the lantern to smother the fire. I stamped on the shawl, broken glass crunching under my feet.

Papa blinked his eyes several times. "Good, Victoria," he whispered. Slowly, he hoisted himself to his feet, pressing his left arm against the wall for a crutch.

My face flushed. "Are you all right, Papa?"

He turned his head toward the sound of churning lake and pelting rain, and I knew he was worrying about boats being lost out there in the dark, unable to see shore.

In a low voice, he said, "I must light the lanterns and wind the winches." The winches were the weights and gears of a machine that turned the Fresnel lens around the lanterns so the light shining through them was very bright. He put his left foot on the first rung. But he couldn't lift his right arm to grasp the side of the ladder. It stayed at his side and wouldn't move. He picked up his right hand with his left. It flopped from his grasp like a wet fish. He cursed, some words in Norwegian, and kicked the ladder.

"Papa, I can do it. I can go up and light it," I got out in a shaky voice. The gusting wind flung a sluice of rain against the windows and lightning flared.

Papa stopped dead. Like he had come out of a trance, he pulled a box of matches from his pocket with his good hand and pushed it at me. "Here, take this up with you."

The six rungs seemed far apart. I pulled myself up as much by my hands as my feet. When I stood on the last rung with my head and half of my body in the lantern room, I gaped at the beehive-shaped glass globe that filled it. I had only seen the Fresnel lens high up from the ground outside and had no idea of its true size. I scrambled onto the floor and stood up. The lens looked like an enormous crystal chandelier in a queen's glass dining room. Once again lightning flashed, and out the window, as plain as midday, I saw a vessel rocking on the high waves close to the island.

"A ship," I screamed.

Papa's captain voice. "You must light the wick. Strike a match against the side of the box and reach inside to the lantern."

I tried three times before a match caught. Papa kept bellowing "Hurry" and "Be careful" and I was terrified I would drop a match and start a new fire. Carefully, I edged a trembling flame behind one prism to the wick. The illuminated glass blazed in a brightness that nearly closed my eyes.

"I did it, Papa."

"Come down, then."

Back in the watch room floor, the storm howled on.

"Now you must help me wind the winches." Papa had lit another lantern and set it down near the clockwork weight that kept the Fresnel lens turning. With his good left arm and both of mine we cranked and cranked, our breaths in rough gasps from the exertion. At last Papa said the machine would run long enough, and we should go downstairs.

The storm had calmed. In the parlor, I crawled on the sofa. "Is the ship safe, Papa?" I asked. In the flickering lantern light, I made out the black square of Mama's piano.

Papa slumped into his chair. "We'll know in the morning."

Tears seeped under my lids and trickled down my cheeks, and I couldn't move. I must have fallen asleep for a few minutes. When I opened my eyes again, the noise of the storm was gone.

"Pa-pa?" I drew out the word like a baby.

There was no answer at first, then he grunted a weak humph, shifting in his chair.

I watched him, thinking of fire. I pictured the lightning dancing for that split second on the ladder. I saw the tongue of the lantern flames licking the floor like a thirsty animal. I wanted to draw it, what I imagined and what I saw. Since Papa had burned my first drawing, I had not dared to make a sketch. Now the vision was overwhelming. Papa was still sleeping. I got up and took his Bible from the table and put the lantern on the table next to the sofa. I opened the Bible across my knees. I turned the pages, looking for verses that said drawing was a sin.

Entry 6 -- 28 Feb. 1868 – Weather: Mixed snow and rain

Dear Joseph,
    What a spirit-numbing day. The chaotic sky from my window the bleakest hues of the painter's palette – gray, black, white, brown...
    A missal with a white cover, worn by many fingers before mine, takes up a corner of my small desk; every woman has a copy in her room. I find no comfort in it. Every week I shift the bookmark to the day's Mass for inspection to satisfy Sister Margaret that I am interested in praising God. Instinct says I must stay on her good side. Yet, I wonder, haven't I always gloried in my endurance of doubt, of fear, even of terror? I won't be defeated.

On My Own
(Shoreside Light, September 1856)

After the night of the fire, Papa hardly spoke. He sat in the living room reading the Bible and muttering to himself between chores, even in the daytime. His burn began to heal, leaving a welt like a purple worm under his skin. A few nights I was awakened by his crying out in his sleep, the words too garbled to understand.

For the first time since Mama had left, a day would go by without her ghost presence on the island. I slept better, though dreaming often of swooning like Joan of Arc amid flames, sometimes trapped, sometimes escaping into the merciful lake water. One morning I picked up Mama's bracelet, which I had left lying on the floor, and poked it into a back corner of the dollhouse.

When Mr. Mackelhorn arrived a week later, Papa escorted him to the lighthouse. They stamped their feet on the rug by the front door. "Sorry about your arm, Willoughby. I'll arrange for a lightning rod to be installed," the inspector said.

Victoria's Quest

I was nervously working at the stove, stirring a fish chowder and peeking in the oven at a pumpkin pie. Mr. Mackelhorn leaned his head into the kitchen. When he saw me, he frowned. "Is Mrs. Willoughby about?"

"Victoria is helping with the cooking chores until Mrs. Willoughby returns from a short visit to her family." Papa's voice trembled. I turned away to lay plates on the table.

The men climbed to the tower for the inspection and then returned to the kitchen for lunch. Without Mama, we ate in near silence. The chowder was over salted, the potatoes hard, and the pie filling as runny as pudding. As soon as he finished, Mr. Mackelhorn stood up with a hurried "Thank you, Miss."

"Will you have a cup of coffee in the parlor?" Papa asked.

"I thank you but not this time," the inspector said quickly. "I'll look forward to my next visit and Mrs. Willoughby's piano playing." He didn't notice the glower on Papa's face.

After the tender left, Papa returned to the parlor and the Bible. "Going out for a bit," I said to no reply.

The air was cold with a biting breeze. I heard a faint honking and looked up to the gray sky. To the north, a moving black vee grew larger and larger, becoming a flock of Canada geese. As they passed over me, screeching, I saw the undersides of their wide dark wings and the clever way their feet tucked under their bodies. I stretched as tall as I could and opened my arms skyward, imagining flying up to them and seeing the island as they did, a circle of green dotted with white squares.

I walked past the coop, the chickens inside squawking at the sound of my footsteps, to the dying vegetable garden and on down to the west side of the island. Here, a short distance north of the boathouse, the shore pushed out in a rocky ledge, a gathering place for the gulls. I squatted and, with a stone, scratched the word *fire* on the smooth oval of a rock. I scratched another word beneath it: *lie.* I was confused about what Papa had told Mr. Mackelhorn about Mama. It was the first lie I had ever heard him tell. *How could Papa lie, Papa who said you must always tell the truth as the Bible says?* Maybe, I thought with sudden hope, he *was* telling the truth, that Mama *was* coming home soon. In the next moment, I knew that couldn't be. *Why would he keep that a secret from me, only to tell Mr. Mackelhorn?*

In the lighthouse, Papa was limping around and around his chair. His uneven gait yanked his torso up and down as if it were on a pulley.

When I interrupted him, he looked at me with burning eyes and said, "The Bible says man and woman were meant to be together. She knows her duty." He punched a fist forward like a boxer.

I stayed at the doorway. "Is Mama going to come back?"

Papa stopped at the piano, pointing at the keyboard. "I thought that would keep her happy. I knew music of that sort was a temptation of the devil. A sin." He frightened me, yet his anger sparked my own.

"Is that why you burned my drawing?" I asked.

He halted. "Yes."

"It's only something I like doing," I said defiantly.

"It will take over your life, Victoria, and make you forget your duty and forget God. I will not have you end up like my father." Papa resumed his angry limping.

Father? Papa had never talked about his father, only his mother. His father died young, in an accident, Mama said, when Papa was a boy.

"What did he do?" I came into the parlor and stood behind the sofa.

"He went to the devil with his crazy doings, and I'm going to make sure you don't. Now that's enough. I've decided what I must do and you, girl, must do your part." Papa stopped in front of his chair and heaved himself into it with a groan.

His words scared and excited me. I braced my hands on the sofa and waited.

"I need to go into Shoreside," he went on. "It will take me twice as long to row with a bum arm, and I won't be able to get back until after dark."

I couldn't take in what he was saying. "Couldn't I help you row?"

Papa rubbed a hand on his thigh. "You're ten, Victoria, and you've lit the lanterns once." He gave me a rare smile.

My heart thumped hard in my chest. He was telling me I was to stay alone, to be in charge of the lighthouse!

"What if someone gets in trouble on the lake," I asked, shivering.

"If the boat's close to shore, you can throw a rope. Otherwise..." Papa shrugged. "There is hardly anything running now, only a few bigger ships passing and they won't sink. Believe me, girl."

I swelled with giddy pride. "Yes, Papa," I said, a sailor obeying the captain.

The whole next day, I practiced what Papa taught me – how to trim the wicks, wipe smoke off the lanterns, wash the tower windows, polish the brass and wash the soot from the Fresnel lens, and hardest of all, wind the winches by myself. Later, he turned the keeper's log to the black-lined page headed SEPTEMBER 1856 and showed me where to record the date and weather. The leather-covered ledger was twice as big as my biggest schoolbook and lay flat when open.

At first light the next morning, Papa set off in the rowboat, pulling each oar with one hand, first one side then the other. I stood in the lighthouse tower in a panic, watching him zigzag out of sight.

My mind seemed separated – Victoria doing, Victoria asleep. I put out the lanterns and cleaned them to be re-lit at night. At Papa's desk, I leafed through several back pages of the log as I hadn't dared to in his presence. I was disappointed there was nothing about our family in it. He recorded only weather, the state of the lighthouse and the equipment, and occasionally the rescue of a boat. From one entry, a name jumped out at me. "Brought in a local named Flanagan who hit the shoals. His boat destroyed. Put him up overnight and returned him to town." Papa didn't say, as I would have, that for once the lighthouse had rung with laughter and music, Mr. Flanagan joking at the breakfast table in a blanket and telling Mama stories and giving me a penny.

In the far right hand of each page was a column titled *Expenses*. Beneath it Papa had listed items from Strachey's deducted from his monthly salary of forty dollars. As I closed the ledger, a loose paper slipped out and the next thing I knew, I was looking, wide-eyed, at a bill for thirty-five dollars, from a Mr. J.J. Rankin. *That was nearly a month's salary! Did he have something to do with Papa's urgent trip to town?* The secret bill frightened me, Papa owing a stranger so much money, Papa who had never given Mama more than a few dollars to spend in town.

I ran downstairs and busied myself with morning chores. Washing and drying the dishes. Carrying the pan of dishwater outside and dumping it in the little flower beds on either side of the front door. The stems of the geraniums had gone raggedy but a few blossoms still held their summer pinkness. I fed the chickens and from the coop out back gathered some eggs to boil for my supper.

In the afternoon, it began to rain and storm clouds were gathering toward town. Had Papa even gotten to Shoreside yet? I worried that he had not been able to keep rowing with one arm. Restless, I picked up blank sheets of school paper and a pencil and carried a lantern to the dark parlor. I dragged the piano bench to use as a board in front of Papa's chair, perched on the edge, and began to draw. *I'm a sinner like Papa's father,* I thought. But right then I didn't care. Anyway, I didn't understand. What did sin have to do with wanting to draw on paper the images in my head? Beneath my fingers appeared a frenzy of strokes – spikes, jags, arcs – the sparks on the ladder, the snake of fire darting across the floor. When I finished, the gusting wind outside and the tempest in my head had eased.

By then it was dusk, and I hurried up the stairs and up into the lantern room. I struck a match and stared for a moment, transfixed by its tiny magical burst of red, before poking it on the lantern wick behind the lens. When the lens glowed with light, I returned to the tower room and opened the log. *"23 Sept., Raining, somewhat windy, but no storm after all,"* I decided to write. Then I set about winding the winches, a task three times harder without Papa there to help. It seemed to take hours to finish turning the crank enough times and my arm muscles burned with pain. Still, the work kept me from thinking about the fact that Papa was not home yet. My stomach rumbled but the thought of my planned egg and bread supper closed my throat. I paced the room, rubbing my arms, and looked out the tower window every few minutes. I couldn't keep my mind on any one thought before it skipped away into blankness. It was getting later and later, the lake barely visible. And, then, finally, there, I spotted in the distance Papa's rowboat jerking toward the island. At last! At last! I ran downstairs, outside, and down the path to the boathouse.

When Papa pulled in, I was standing next to the boathouse, sobbing with relief.

"Now, now, girl," he said, clamping his good arm around my shoulder. "Let's get out of this dratted rain." His raw face, a mottled red above his black slicker, looked as miserable to me as my tear-swollen one must have to him. But we had both survived.

Entry 7 -- 29 Feb. 1868 – Weather: Cold and sunny

Dear Joseph,

    I'm in St. Mary's Haven for unwed mothers and have been with child for six months. I'm ready to record these facts as plainly as Papa observed the passing of ships in his log. Until now, I haven't wanted to admit how poorly I felt even to myself – keeping down little food from meals, moving around in a half-stupor during the day after a long night of broken sleep and nightmares, cramping in sudden sharp pains, often full of dread when I wake in the morning. But I want so much to bear this baby! Sister Margaret and Mother Superior are experienced midwives who attend labor and delivery with Doctor Stephens called only if there are complications. I don't know how much help Sister Margaret will be with her useless arm...

    But I'm cheered today, somehow feel better able to manage, after the unexpected discovery of a wonderful painting. I should note, decoration in St. Mary's Haven is absent except for religious images, paintings of a bearded, white-robed, glowing Jesus preaching on a hillside or laying hands on the sick, and of saints often in a state of martyrdom. I particularly detest the one above the parlor fireplace of St. Jerome with his torso bloodied and pierced by arrows like a deer tortured by cruel hunters. Still, it's probably no more painful for the girls to look at than the statue of Madonna and Child at the end of the front hall.

    Anyway, I had not realized a painting hung on the wall behind the dining room door, which nearly always stands open. This morning as I passed by, the door was closed and I stopped in mid-step at the sudden burst of bright colors and figures before my eyes. For some minutes, I stood riveted in the hall, absorbing the details with my artist's eye. Across the wide canvas sprawled a panoramic scene of a boisterous market day in a town square – farmers with cows and pigs and chickens, hawkers with stalls of vegetables and fruit,

41

townspeople, mainly women, moving among them with baskets, children running everywhere, most of the faces red, smiling, open-mouthed. The painting was so alive!

And there, in the foreground, stood a young soldier in blue holding the reins of his palomino and bowing toward a young woman in a red shawl, a basket of eggs over her arm. As I gazed at them, a dizziness engulfed me and the rest of the painting emptied out, the way it did when I brushed white paint over discarded images in my own work. I saw only the young couple, a drama between them about to happen, and then Paul Willoughby stood before me, hands in his pockets, grinning and talking in that too quick way of his.

My thoughts went back to that more innocent time in my life, when hope for the future was born, a hope I long to regain.

Here I had to stop writing for a few minutes, overcome by the odor of boiled mutton seeping like poison fumes under my door. I vomited in the washbowl and, after emptying it in the privy, scrubbed it and my face and my mouth clean of the liquid sourness in a near frenzy. So I won't go to the dining room for Sister Barbara's noon meal. I will sit here, the window cracked open for fresh air, and burrow into a memory of the past.

Cousin
(Shoreside, April 1857)

Cousin Sherman told Papa the previous fall that we were to have noon dinner at his house on our first trip to Shoreside in the spring. On a clear April Saturday, we rowed in and headed to the Willoughby's three-story limestone house on Front Street.

Sally, the big, plump-legged farm girl who worked as the maid, opened the door. A tantalizing smell of fried chicken filled the air as she showed us to the library alcove behind the drawing room. I hadn't seen this part of the house before. I was enchanted by my first view: a glass-fronted bookcase of leather-bound volumes and above it a gold-framed painting of a formal, white-pillared building against a backdrop of soft pinks and blues.

Near a small window, Cousin Abigail was writing notes at a desk in a full-skirted, tight-bodiced dress of silky maroon with a wide lace collar. Glancing up at our worn clothes and faces, she said, "You must be nearly mad from being penned up like animals all winter." Deftly, she blotted the ink on her paper.

"Hello, Cousin Abigail. I hope the family has been well," Papa said.

"Very well," she said in a way that suggested impatience. She picked up a silver hand bell and shook it.

"Ask Rose to prepare two extra places," she told Sally when the maid appeared.

"If it's not too much trouble." Papa pulled himself up from the lopsided stance that favored his bad leg.

"Sherman will be here shortly," Cousin Abigail replied.

As if he had heard her cool tone, her husband almost immediately arrived to join us.

"How delightful to see you, Victoria and Edward!" he boomed, beaming down at me and clapping Papa's shoulder. The two men crushed hands.

Their fathers were brothers, and the cousins had in common their height and directness of gaze. Yet Sherman's face was fat and Papa's lean. Sherman's voice honked like a goose whereas Papa's voice rumbled from someplace deep in his chest. Sherman kept up a stream of talk in one visit that would have taken Papa a year to put forth.

The four of us proceeded to the dining room, crowded with dark, gleaming furniture. I was impressed to see the bottoms of the table legs looked like lion's paws. Paul, the younger son, was already there, standing at his place. He said hello to Papa and me. I dipped my head. I hardly remembered him from one year to the next, but this time seeing him felt different.

Papa and I sat opposite Paul with his parents at either end. As I took my place, I was surprised to see in the polished front of the sideboard my father's serious expression on my own face.

"Sit down, folks," Cousin Sherman urged. "Michael's a foreman now and won't be with us. He puts in a full work day on Saturdays." Behind him, the window was open to the fresh spring breeze. Through it, I drank in the green backyard with bursts of red tulips and yellow daffodils and beyond them the sparkling blue of the lake.

Then I gazed at the bounty before me so unlike our meals at the lighthouse. A fine white lace cloth draped the table, which was set with gold-edged china and crowded with platters and bowls of steaming, delicious looking food. Children did not speak unless spoken to during meals. I didn't mind, I was glad to eat my way through a plateful of chicken pieces, tender red-skinned potatoes, and crisp spring asparagus and listen to Cousin Sherman wander through his stories.

Victoria's Quest

It sounded familiar, what he started talking about, the founding of his railroad car company. He probably had told the same story when we were here before, the last time we were with Mama.

"Yes, Edward, you were already at sea when I left home at eighteen to strike out on my own," he said, adding a thick slice of bread to his plate. "I saw the railroads coming and I seized my opportunity in Shoreside with Willoughby's Railroad Manufacturing Company. I know people call it Willie's. That's all right with me," he laughed, "as long as it makes me good money."

"You've done well, Sherman, for a landlubber." Papa surprised me, daring to joke at his cousin's expense.

"Indeed, indeed." Cousin Sherman was busy buttering his bread. He looked down the table and smiled at his wife. "Of course, it was as hard as starting Willie's to persuade Abigail here to marry me and move to Indiana after she graduated from the Patapsco Academy for Young Ladies."

Cousin Abigail took a sip of water. "I miss the more civilized ways of the East. But I *have* tried to establish a semblance of it here with the more prominent ladies of Shoreside through my literary discussion group and play reading club."

"And it's been a wonderful contribution and service, my dear, much appreciated by the citizens," her husband said.

Cousin Abigail nodded and glanced around the table.

In the brief silence, cutlery clicked on plates, jaws worked, and throats swallowed. I saw Paul sneaking looks at me across the table.

Cousin Sherman cleared his throat. "Did you know, Edward, there's a special kind of railroad coming through Indiana these days?"

Papa raised his eyebrows. "What's that?" He was eating as hungrily as I was and already taking seconds.

"It's called the underground railroad. Not a real train, of course, but houses and barns of safety for Negro slaves escaping from the South up to Canada."

"That's a fine, Christian thing to do," Papa said.

"Sherman has suggested our home, but I don't think..." Cousin Abigail trailed off.

"Other Shoresiders are hiding them already, my dear," Cousin Sherman said quickly. He looked around the table. "In any event, there's going to be a war about this, the North against the South, before we're done with it," he declared.

"I think you may be right," Papa agreed.

Sally came in and moved around the table, replenishing food. Under her armpits, wide circles of sweat sponged her gingham dress. Paul caught my eye and winked. I had begun giggling when Cousin Sherman suddenly bellowed, "Victoria, how would you like to go to school in town?"

I jerked my head toward him, not sure I'd heard right.

"Can't afford it." Papa answered for me, rolling a spear of asparagus across his plate.

"You don't have to, Edward," Cousin Sherman said. "A new state law's been passed that every town has to have a public school. I've been appointed district superintendent, you know, so I'm in charge of opening one here." He helped himself to another chicken leg.

"When?" I asked.

"September. Mr. Eliot, it so happens, has up and decided to close the academy and seek his fortune in the Dakota Territories. I'm taking it over for an elementary school."

Cousin Abigail sniffed. "I doubt if a public school can provide the education of a private academy for our son. Michael is lucky to have matriculated already."

"Paul will do well. You get along with people, don't you, son?" Cousin Sherman said. "And with animals, too, for that matter. You must show Victoria your new pony."

"Yes, Father," Paul said.

I hoped there would be no opportunity to do so today. I was still afraid of horses.

With gusto, Cousin Sherman bit into the meaty part of the chicken leg and continued. "Already hired two teachers, Mr. Briscoe and Mr. Cartwright. This summer we'll put in a second stove and divide the room into half for four grades each."

"I'd like to go," I said more loudly than I intended.

"Of course you would." Uncle Sherman turned to Papa. "She can live with us, Edward. You two are family. And I've always wanted a girl around the house."

At the other end of the table, Cousin Abigail pressed her thin lips over her plate and cut a boiled potato into dainty cubes. Paul winked at me again, this time with a wide smile. Beside me, Papa stiffened.

"That's very good of you," he said, "but I don't know if Victoria needs more schooling."

"How would it look if my own cousin's daughter didn't go to the new public school?" Uncle Sherman said, unsmiling, raising an eyebrow.

Papa did not reply, and his pale cheeks flushed. The matter was settled.

In the midst of my confused excitement over this new development, I heard the echo of Mama's often repeated words: *I was so glad to get off that farm and move to Shoreside when I could get a job.* Maybe I was more like her than I thought.

The past few months of lighthouse life had been a misery. After the lighthouse tender made its early December stop – this time Papa told Mr. Mackelhorn that Mama had been ill and was recuperating in town – the island became a prison and Papa the silent jailer. One morning I found the piano covered with an old blanket. Papa recovered the use of his arm but limped as badly as ever. I could hardly remember the Papa who had joked about the alligator in the boathouse and read aloud stories about Viking heroes, the Papa who had leaned on me during that stormy night of lightning and fire and later left me in charge one whole day. Often, the ghost at the top of the stairs came to me as I huddled in my bed, soon after Papa started snoring.

When dinner at the Willoughbys was over, Papa said we had to hurry to Strachey's for supplies and then to the boat to row home in time to light the lanterns.

"What's it like going to Shoreside Academy?" I managed to whisper to Paul as the adults said goodbye at the door.

"It's all right except Mr. Eliot hits us with a switch if we don't answer right."

"Oh, no," I said out loud.

Paul grinned. "Don't worry, the teachers don't whip girls."

"What subjects do you like best?" I asked.

"History and geography," he said. "I love reading about wars and far-off places. As soon as I'm old enough, I'm going to see the world."

See the world. It was such a big idea I couldn't get the words out of my head as Papa and I walked to Strachey's. *See the world, see the world.*

Entry 8 -- 2 Mar. 1868 – Weather: Very windy

Dear Joseph,

On my way to sewing class, I hovered a minute or two by the mail table in the front hall. Every morning, no matter how poorly I feel, I risk being caught looking through the mail. Anything for the girls is collected and read by Mother Superior (one of the rules of St. Mary's Haven) and I must intercept any reply to that frantic letter I wrote the day I arrived. Oh, how much I hoped today was the day I would hear for the sake of my baby! My heart pounding, I saw a plain white envelope with writing in a clear, graceful hand. This could be it! But no. The address was to a Sister Margaret Kelly and had Irish postal stamps. Dennis Kelly's letter must have crossed with the one I wrote for the nun a few days ago. Frustrated, hardly realizing what I was doing, I slipped the letter in my sleeve and hurried into the parlor.

The girls are required to attend two hours of communal sewing three times a week while Sister Rosamund stalks irritably behind our chairs, looking over our shoulders at our efforts. We make infant clothes – blankets, sleeping gowns, and caps. Sister Rosamund has given up on my doing anything other than turn hems on blankets. I'm as hopeless at sewing as I've always been at cooking. I don't understand how my fingers confidently wield a pencil or brush but turn clumsy and stiff working a needle. Sister Rosamund says, "I'm sure you are glad to be useful and to supply garments for poor families the Church is helping." I believe they will be used for our own babies, the ones we bear and give up a day after birth. A few of the others must believe that, too, for they have tears in their eyes as they sew.

When Sister Rosamund released us, I escaped to my room, thinking of Mama. Rubbing my fingers over the bracelet, which has become loose on my wrist in the past weeks, the rustle in my sleeve reminded me of Dennis Kelly's letter. I pulled it out, using my fingers like an iron to smooth out the wrinkled paper on my desk and ease open the envelope.

Victoria's Quest

The warmth and intimacy of his letter did not surprise me, knowing how desperately Sister Margaret cared about communicating with him. After remarks about the wet cold weather and the smokiness of peat fires in his cousin's house, he wrote: *Please tell me the truth, dear Margaret, about your well-being. I worry about you.* So, Sister Margaret has been as secretive about herself in all her letters as the one I wrote for her. I read on, wondering at the meaning behind his next words: *This work is becoming too heavy a penance. At your age, you have paid enough for your sins.*

I paused. *Sins.* One of Papa's favorite words; I think of fire when I hear it, not the fire of hell but of the stove and Papa burning my drawing. But it's hard to picture Sister Margaret as a sinner.

I skimmed the rest of the letter. By the time she received this, he wrote, he'll be on his way home to Chicago. He's enjoyed himself but feels he's outworn his welcome and told all the stories of their parents he can remember and heard all of the stories of Ireland he can stand. Besides, he misses the school boys. The letter closed with love and admonitions to take care of herself in the meantime.

Still vexed about not receiving my own letter, I thrust hers in the small drawer of my desk. I wouldn't try to return it to the mail table before lunch as I had planned, I thought peevishly. Let Sister Margaret do without it another day.

Angrily, I sat down to add another entry to my log.

One about the summer before I moved to Cousin Sherman's house, when I received a letter, one that hardened my heart with an inner rage which, despite all that's happened, has never quite left me.

Mama's Letter
(Shoreside, July 1857)

Mama sent a letter by way of Maggie Fogarty, who gave it to me with a sad hug on a July visit to town. I was eleven and Mama had been gone a year. I ran through the streets to the beach where I was to wait for Papa and sat on the dock, reading the words with shaking hands and blurred eyes. There was a Chicago postmark but no return address.

> *Dear Victoria,*
> *I hope you are well and helping Papa with*
> *the lighthouse. Someday I hope you understand*

why I had to leave. Believe me, it's better
for you to be with your father there than with
me in my life here. You would not like it. I am
not the mother you should have. I tried but I
couldn't live on that island. Maybe we can meet
one day when you are grown.
              Love, Mama

Mama's writing tilted every which way on the small sheet of rough brown paper. I read it over and over, my damp hands smearing the ink. *Why did Mama think I would understand?* She was not the Mama who had lived with us, she was some other woman, someone I didn't want to know. I got up and stumbled off the dock onto shore. I stalked up and down the beach, kicking up sand and glaring at the shimmering blue lake.

When Papa arrived, I stuffed the letter in my pocket, and after we got back to the island I burned the letter in the stove. That night in the parlor, I told Papa that Maggie Fogarty had word that Mama was well and living in Chicago but that's all she or anyone else knew. He got up from his chair without a word and went up to wind the winches.

The rest of the summer as I went about my chores and waited for school to open, my mind lived in the cruelest parts of my fairy tale books – kings who had court jesters beheaded, forced their daughters to marry ugly old men, ordered soldiers into battle against hopeless odds. I imagined myself a man in these fantasies because the person with power always seemed to be a king or knight or giant. In my room, when I knew Papa was outdoors, I copied scenes of soldiers clashing with swords, giants tramping through villages, peasants whipping oxen in fields. Every stroke of my pencil took me into the story where I exulted with the merciless victors. I felt sick to my stomach when I finished a drawing but I couldn't stop.

In the end, I tore up and fed all the drawings into the kitchen stove except one, a knight on a horse stabbing a dragon. I hid that one inside the piano, laying it atop the dusty strings. I knew Papa would not come upon it there.

Entry 9 -- 3 Mar. 1868 -- Weather: Unseasonably warm

Dear Joseph,

I've always felt like an outsider. It's no different here at St. Mary's Haven. When I was a child, the only girls I didn't feel apart from were Maggie Fogarty's daughters. I fell in so naturally to being part of their lives that I didn't have a chance to wonder whether I was accepted or not.

Here, I know the women visit each other in their rooms. When I pass down the hall I hear giggling and talking like schoolgirls. I wish I could put more firmly out of my mind, as they seem to, thoughts of the immediate future and the unknown after that, the years when we are to begin a "new" life.

Elise, who arrived yesterday as the eighth pregnant girl, appears to be different. Her eyes are a startling butterscotch in an oval face framed by black ringlets. Though statuesque, she moves with the ease of a dancer. What a beautiful portrait she would make! Her clothes and manner suggest she comes from wealth, as did the ladies whose likenesses I painted in what seems like a lifetime ago. She looks like she ought to be resting on a damask sofa in the drawing room of a mansion with servants hovering around her, awaiting the birth of her child in pampered comfort. Perhaps that's why she holds herself a bit aloof from the rest of us.

As we left the dining hall after lunch, I walked next to her and said quietly, "Hello, Elise."

"Oh." With a start, she turned and looked over, I should say down, at me. "Hello, Victoria."

"Would you like to join me for a walk outdoors?" How stilted my words sounded even to my own ears.

A flicker of surprise passed over her face before it returned to its calm expression. "Thank you, but I thought I would rest now. Perhaps another day soon." Her smile seemed genuine but she increased her pace and moved on before I could say anything else.

Victoria's Quest

I turned back angrily and headed directly out to the street, the sun bathing my face with warmth that matched the heat of my emotions. *Oh, yes, Victoria,* I thought. *Don't forget others may feel as uneasy in your company as you do in theirs.*

I took an hour's walk, despite the cramps that came on shortly after I began. I ventured east to the lake and walked south along the lakefront. Here, the wind cleansed the air of the worst odors of garbage and manure. I kept my eyes on the swaying waves of the gray-blue water, my body absorbing the light wind, and paused often to take deep breaths of fresh air. The sky was a canopy of azure, ornamented with some high white clouds. The brightness everywhere lifted my spirits.

Back in my room, my stomach calmer as I write this, I think again of being an outsider. Elise reminds me of Cousin Abigail, who always sought to keep me one. At school I was an outsider, too. But I did have Paul, then, as I will always have you, Joseph.

School
(Shoreside, September 1857)

The day Papa left me at Cousin Sherman's, his wife's first words were, "My husband invited you to live here, Victoria, against my wishes." Cousin Abigail was watching me unpack my meager belongings from Papa's old trunk in the tiny room across from Sally's and Rose's quarters on the third floor.

I sensed no response was welcome and hung a dress on a hook along the wall.

"I trust you will behave yourself and offer no trouble to my household," she went on, waving a vague hand in my direction. "You will be given chores, of course, and I will train you in manners. I'm sure you'll need that, being out on that island and away from a woman's influence in how a young lady conducts herself."

"Yes, Cousin Abigail," I said, imagining a scrawny witch pointing a skinny finger in place of her image in the doorway.

She must have heard something in my tone for she said, "I can't understand how a woman can leave her husband, let alone a child." She arched pale eyebrows over her narrow eyes. "I suppose being Irish and a farm girl explains it, although I can't imagine even Sally doing that, if someone comes along to marry her."

At these words, I willed expression out of my face, a look I adopted whenever after that she delivered such remarks.

Shoreside Public School, formerly Mr. Eliot's Academy, was located south of Front Street and several streets east of Main. On a warm September day, Paul and I set off early for the opening of school. The air smelled of manure as we passed houses where cows and pigs were penned in sheds and yards. When I shied away from the horses eyeing us and tossing their heads close to the fences next to our path, Paul grinned. "You won't be afraid of my Sandy, Victoria." I saw no reason why I wouldn't be.

Over the noise of the streets came the din of the mills and factories. Men's voices shouted over sawing, hammering, the clank and whir of machinery, and the creak and clunk of crates being hoisted onto wagons. We knew much of the activity was at Willie's. "We can barely keep up with companies wanting rail cars with all the train lines coming into Indiana and other states," Paul said as if he were a partner in his father's operation.

I stopped and dusted off the front of my dress when we got to the front gate of the school, a handsome brick house set back from the street. The school bell tolled in rhythm with my pounding heart.

"Come on, you're a Willoughby," Paul said, as I watched the other students approaching. My heart sank at the girls' pretty dresses and hair bows. I had only my old blue dress and bonnet to wear until Cousin Abigail's seamstress arrived next month to make clothes for the family. The two male teachers stood at the door and asked ages, pointing to a classroom either to the left or right.

Paul and I were sent to Mr. Briscoe's class, fourth through sixth grades. We took places as we wished on the benches, Paul and I in the back, until the teacher arrived. Mr. Briscoe was a short, round man with a neatly trimmed dark beard and round, wire-framed spectacles. He reminded me of a plump owl as he blinked at the sunlight from the windows and strutted to the front of the room. He mounted a raised platform that displayed a large wood desk and perched in his chair. Behind him on the wall hung a blackboard with rows of words written in chalk. He took our names, entered them into a roll book, and decided on our grade level.

When Paul called out his name, Mr. Briscoe smiled. "On to sixth level, Master Willoughby." When I said my name next, he looked up and swiveled his head until he saw my raised hand.

"How old are you, Miss Willoughby?"

Victoria's Quest

"Ten."

"You are small to be ten, but I'll try you at fifth level."

Somewhere in the room was a stifled giggle.

The class numbered nineteen, twelve boys and seven girls. Mr. Briscoe assigned us places on the benches, the youngest students in front. Paul sat in the last row on the left. I was given a place at the very end of a bench in the middle by the window. The girl to my left had rosy cheeks and curly brown hair. She shifted her body away from me and whispered to the blond girl next to her whenever Mr. Briscoe wasn't looking. I turned to look out the window, at the houses across the street, and, above their roofs, the sky and clouds.

We were all to copy and memorize spelling words for our grade level from the blackboard. I bent over my paper until recess. Mr. Briscoe first sent the girls to the privy out back, then the boys, then everyone had free time for another ten minutes. Paul and several other boys ran in circles, slapping each other's legs with their caps. I took a breath and walked over to two girls who sat next to me.

"Hello, I'm Victoria Willoughby." I forced a smile, feeling my cheeks tremble.

"I heard. You and Paul must be in the same family," said the one with brown curly hair. "I'm Charlotte Dewey."

"I'm Sarah Tansley," the other girl said. She had a broad nose and her fine blond hair glistened like corn silk in the sun.

"My father is the lighthouse keeper. I'm living in town at my cousin's house," I said.

The girls looked at each other. "I heard your mother ran away," Sarah said, twisting a finger in a curl.

"That's not true. She got sick and died," I said, turning away, fury reddening my face. I hurried back inside to my place on the bench and looked out the window when Charlotte and Sarah returned.

As the first week passed, all the girls ignored me. I was sure Charlotte and Sarah passed the word to do so. Paul was no help. Boys and girls did not mix during the school day. After a while I stayed in during recess, too proud to try further to make friends. On the back of old school papers, I secretly sketched the world outside the school window. I told myself I didn't need friends. The present didn't matter, only the future, when I would be an artist. Leaving the island by going to school was the first step to what I wanted.

Once in a while, I drew comfort from a Saturday visit to the Fogartys. Patricia and Bridget were too old for school, being fourteen and thirteen. Peter was in Mr. Briscoe's class and Sean, who was not quite five, would go to Mr. Cartwright's class next year. The newest Fogarty, Anna, had been born in September. She was small and listless, unlike her robust brothers and sisters. Aunt Maggie kept her crib in the warm kitchen and whenever she had a spare moment, she sat at the table, crooning and singing to Anna while she sewed pieces in another quilt. "Lord help me, this is sometimes a hard life," she would sigh and in the next moment hug whichever child wandered in.

Paul and I mainly saw each other at dinner and talked while walking back and forth from school. He was always looking beyond the horizon, not wanting to see anything unpleasant in the little world of Shoreside, such as the way his mother treated me. "When I ride Sandy on the beach, I feel like I could go all the way around Lake Michigan up to Canada. What do you suppose that would be like?" he'd sing out. Or, waving his arms, "How I'd like to go wherever the new trains go when they leave the yard, Victoria!"

Cousin Sherman was absorbed in his business at Willie's, local politics, and unceasing speculation about a coming war. He left the running of the household entirely to Cousin Abigail. At dinner, he liked to question me as well as Paul about what we had learned that day. Whatever we reported, he always said, "Very good, very good," as if taking credit for our knowledge. Then he would ramble on to Cousin Abigail about who he'd seen that day and talk to Michael, who was quiet and had a drooping moustache, about the Rebellion, as he called it, of the South against becoming a united country and freeing the slaves. "We must have a union of citizens of the whole nation," he would declare, thumping his fist on the table while Michael nodded and Paul's eyes shone with excitement.

"A war would be dreadful," Cousin Abigail would say in a high-pitched voice, but no one seemed to hear her.

On Sundays, Cousin Sherman rented an enormous cream mare named Storm and a roofed carriage from the Fifth Street livery stable for

Victoria's Quest

the family to ride in style to St. Andrews Episcopal Church on the west end of Shoreside. I was glad to be excused from attending on account of not being a member. "I guess you are still Catholic," Cousin Abigail said dubiously. "But then your father is the religious one and he's Lutheran." I watched from my third floor window as Storm tossed her head and started off with her brisk clip-clop.

When they returned, there was a long Sunday dinner. Near the end of one such meal in mid-November, I was sleepily finishing a piece of apple pie when Cousin Sherman suddenly turned to me. "Well, Victoria, how do you like that fine horse of Paul's? A half-breed, of course, but the stallion was a thoroughbred."

"He's nice," I said cautiously.

"*She.*" Paul grinned. "Sandy is a mare. And you haven't even come to visit her once, Victoria, since you've been here!"

"You and that horse, Paul. You certainly spend enough time with her," Michael teased, twisting his moustache.

"Well, why haven't you, Victoria?" Cousin Sherman demanded. "You've time after school." His voice boomed, which meant he was in an especially good mood.

"Victoria spends much time on her homework," Cousin Abigail said, giving me a stern look.

"Very good, very good." Cousin Sherman nodded. "Well, then, this afternoon is the perfect opportunity. Paul, you take Victoria out to meet Sandy. She'd like a new friend, I'm sure." Cousin Sherman honked his laugh. I wasn't sure whether he meant the horse or me.

Sandy was kept in a paddock at the southern edge of the Willoughby's Front Street property next to a small barn with a milk cow and some chickens. Cousin Sherman employed a skinny boy named Tom from the livery stable to feed, water, and groom her. Sandy was ready for Paul to ride any day or time he fancied.

I walked slowly through the back yard behind Paul, who had brought a few apples in his pocket. A brisk wind swirled around us. Well before we reached the open-railed fence, Sandy was straining against it, her head thrust over the top.

"She smells food," Paul laughed. He stepped close and patted the side of the horse's face. She lowered her head, nosing around his pockets. "Hey, Sandy, old girl, how are you today?"

I stayed to one side, looking out toward the lake, feeling the horse loom above me like a brown mountain. "Why do you call her Sandy?" I asked to cover my fear. "She doesn't have any yellow color." As if

56

understanding what I'd said, she turned her head and eyed me. The whites of her eyes seemed enormous.

"Oh, I know she's a bay, but I named her that because she loves to roll in the sand on the beach." Paul pulled out an apple and grinned as she worked it noisily with her teeth. Loose pieces of apples dropped from her mouth to the ground. He wagged his head. "Sloppier than a pig. Here's another apple. How about you feeding her?"

"She doesn't know me." What a silly thing to say.

"Here's how you get acquainted then. Tom showed me." Paul blew gently into the horse's nostrils. "Horses like that. That's how they say hello to each other. So if people do that, horses know you're friendly."

In spite of my fear, I was fascinated by the idea of horses having a secret language. As I took Paul's place, Sandy shifted a few steps, her ears back, then quieted with a soft nicker when I blew into her nostrils. I held the apple under her mouth. Immediately, the horse's lips swept across my palm and lifted up the treat. "Her mouth is soft. It tickles." My hand floated up and patted the horse's warm neck.

Entry 10 -- 7 Mar. 1868 — Weather: Colder, but still bright

Dear Joseph,

This morning I was to tidy the room for inspection. Instead I sat at the desk with the log and turned back to the beginning page of this written journey. Fanning the pages of black script, the events of the past sped faster and faster like a horse breaking from a trot into a canter. There arose in me suddenly a powerful urge to draw. Without thinking, I rose and stepped to the wardrobe, took out the small supply case inside my otherwise empty trunk, and set it on my desk next to the opened log. I looked at the blank page, which had become a painter's canvas awaiting an image.

I unclasped the bracelet from my wrist and held it up before me, admiring once again the delicate silver patterns and pale glittering amethysts. Gently, I lowered it on the table to form a three-layered circle small enough for a baby's wrist. Half hypnotized, I opened the case and took out a piece of charcoal. My hand hovered over the paper, making phantom strokes in the air, before finally moving down to the paper to draw the first line. The paper was thin and slick, not good for drawing. I barely noticed in my joy at once again creating a vision on paper something that touched my heart. The challenge I set for myself was to make the three distinct circles of the bracelet look natural in that arrangement. My first effort was hopeless. I tore out a page and began again. I was so lost in my work that I didn't hear the knock on the door.

Suddenly Sister Margaret was standing next to my desk, saying, "Did you forget inspection, Victoria?" Her face was a prism of light from the sun striking her glasses through the window.

Quickly, I turned the log face down and stood up. My breath caught, she had so surprised me. "I'm – I'm sorry, Sister. Might you check someone else's room and come back to me?"

"That would be all right. You've proven yourself trustworthy," she said as if that had been my question. She moved with unusual energy toward the door. I remembered that yesterday I had watched for the mail delivery and slipped her brother's letter among the other envelopes. She must have received it and been cheered by the news of his return.

Opening the door, she added softly, her back to me so I barely heard the muffled words, "You have a wonderful talent, Victoria."

After I'd done my chores, and she'd come and gone again, with nothing but an exchange of pleasantries between us, I finished the bracelet drawing. I thought it not yet good but not so bad for my being out of practice. When I turned the page, I saw my heavy strokes had nearly pressed through the paper. I remembered I still had a small cache of funds that could be used to buy some sheets of good drawing paper.

The notion cheering me, I thought of Cousin Abigail's surprising gift that temporarily softened the misery of being under her thumb those many years ago, as Sister Margaret's compliment had done the same this morning.

Drawing Supplies
(Shoreside, November 1857)

Cousin Abigail treated me like another servant performing chores on her strict schedule: Monday, washing; Tuesday, ironing; Wednesday, mending and sewing; Thursday, miscellaneous; Friday, cleaning; and Saturday, baking. Sundays no one was supposed to work, only go to church, eat a big noon dinner, and rest.

Though I didn't get back to the house from school until after four o'clock, there was always work for me. On Mondays, most of the clothes Sally had washed in tubs early in the morning were dry by late afternoon. I folded and put away towels, dish rags, sheets, undergarments, and anything else that wasn't to be ironed. On Tuesdays, Rose heated the heavy iron on the cook stove in the kitchen, and I pressed my dresses and other items Cousin Abigail wasn't particular about, such as handkerchiefs.

I dreaded Wednesdays. Mama had done the mending. After she left, Papa, with his sailor's training, had from time to time sewn up the biggest tears in our clothing. Now, I had to help Sally sew up rips in garments and darn holes in stockings. Though I detested this activity, I liked sitting side by side in the upstairs sewing room with the good-natured maid who hummed as she deftly redid my mistakes. She also let me look through the rag bag for colorful quilting scraps that I could give to Maggie Fogarty the next time I saw her.

I was also thrilled to at last have new clothes. In October the seamstress, Mrs. DeWitt, moved in for two weeks. A thin widow who dressed solely in dark dresses with lace collars, she had, said Cousin Abigail, "a very refined French background." Under Cousin Abigail's orders, Mrs. DeWitt made for me a slip and two plain wool dresses with matching bonnets.

On some Wednesdays, Cousin Abigail sighed and attempted to give me sewing lessons in the parlor. "Every respectable girl should be able to demonstrate her skills in the domestic arts," she declared. In my hands, the knitting needles became two uncontrollable wooden sticks I randomly poked together to hook loops of yarn. I dropped and added rows of uneven stitches, never knowing I did so until Cousin Abigail stopped to inspect an hour's work and threw up her hands at the mess. I worked for weeks on a gray wool winter scarf for Paul that she found so unsatisfactory she said I must wear it instead.

I was worse yet at what Cousin Abigail considered most important, needlepoint. My spirit balked at following a pattern and controlling my fingers, endlessly pushing a needle in and out of the canvas instead of sweeping my hand with a pencil across the paper to create a form of my own fancy. The linen became soiled and the thread grubby from the frequent ripping out of stitches that did not meet Cousin Abigail's approval.

Thursdays being for odds and ends, I was often set to cleaning the silver. With Rose's homemade polish, I daubed, wiped off, and rubbed to clear shine the silver platters, serving dishes, tea service, and cutlery. Sometimes Cousin Abigail stood in the dining room and explained the etiquette of a lady entering and exiting a room, sitting and eating. I bit my lip to hold back laughter at her exaggerated movements.

On Friday, cleaning day, I helped Sally change all the beds. Then I swept out my room and the upstairs hall. Cousin Abigail also delighted in asking me to clean the oil lamps. "You're so skilled in that dirty task, my dear, from your upbringing in a lighthouse," she said. Even knowing it was an insult, I scoured the lamps, trimmed the wicks, and polished the glass chimneys until they shone and there was not a speck of dirt left.

Saturdays I spent in the sweet yeasty clatter of the kitchen with Rose, perpetually red-faced but in her best mood of the week. She was not much taller than me and her solid and shapeless torso reminded me of an upended log on legs. Despite her bulk, she moved quickly, her face sweating and her apron strings loosening as she worked. Like Sally, she came from a farming family. Her husband had gone West a year ago to stake a claim on land and would send for her when he was settled. "Baking settles my nerves," she often said while I washed bowls and utensils and fetched flour, salt, sugar, yeast, eggs, and spices. Hour after hour, she rotated trays and pans through the cook stove to turn out the week's supply of bread, rolls, cakes, and pies for the family. She was too nervous and hurried to teach me what she was doing, which suited me, as long as I got samples of the results. Rose was much taken with a new cookbook, *The New Household Receipt Book,* by the same lady who edited Cousin Abigail's treasured magazine, *Godey's Lady's Book.* Cousin Abigail was delighted when Rose presented one of Miss Hale's fashionable recipes to the family.

As for Paul's chores, he was supposed to bring in wood and coal for the cook stove and go to Strachey's to fetch things for Rose or his mother. He was rarely within calling distance. After school he was either riding Sandy or over at his father's factory watching the cars being built. Cousin Abigail scolded him now and then before dinner.

"I'm truly sorry, Mother," he'd say, somehow managing at the same time to sigh, hang his head, and put on a charming smile. For a week, he would industriously run errands and do her bidding and then go back to his old ways.

Many times at night, I couldn't go to sleep until I drew for a while at my bedside table on whatever scraps of paper I could find. I drew what I could make out by candlelight – my hairbrush, the washbowl and pitcher, a dress on a peg or, out the window, the outline of the lighthouse tower with its bright yellow at the top. This was the time I thought most about Papa and even missed him, knowing he was all alone. I hoped the ghost did not trouble him. Often, I had to ask Sally for new candles to replace the ones I had burned down. "I can't see, you being a girl, why you need to stay up late studying," she said, shaking her head. "You're lucky Mrs. Willoughby doesn't count her stores that often."

One night, I heard too late Cousin Abigail's voice in the hall talking to Rose about a dinner party that Cousin Sherman had suddenly decided on for the next evening. Before I could snuff out the candle, my door was pushed open.

"I saw light in here. What are you doing awake at this hour?" Cousin Abigail asked.

"I'm sorry. I'll go to bed now," I said, hastily moving to slip the drawing of the lighthouse under my schoolbooks.

Too late. Cousin Abigail crossed the room and took it from my hand, holding her candle close to it.

"You drew this, Victoria?"

"Yes, Ma'am." I winced at the sharpness of her voice.

"Are you homesick for the lighthouse?"

Yes or no, which is the right answer, I wondered. "It's a pretty scene at night from this window. Please don't tell Papa that..."

"And why not?" she interrupted.

"He doesn't think drawing is a proper Christian activity."

"Oh?" Cousin Abigail continued to stare at my drawing, frowning and tapping her finger on the paper. I held my breath. Finally she said, "Who taught you to draw like this?"

"No one, Cousin Abigail. I like to draw on my own."

She was half-listening, still tapping her finger. "This material is not fit to draw on."

I blinked at her next words.

"I've done some drawing, you know. My final pen-and-ink for the Patapsco Academy hangs in the library downstairs." In the candlelight, Cousin Abigail's face softened.

Instantly, I knew what she meant. "Oh, the fancy white building that hangs over the bookcase."

"The opera house," she corrected. Her voice slowed and became dreamy. "I sketched for hours across the street from that opera house. Not very ladylike out in public but our teacher chaperoned us."

As I was on the verge of asking her more, she snapped to the present, pressed back her shoulders, and said, "Now, don't go reaching beyond your station in life, Victoria."

One evening of the following week, I found a large pad of beautiful white paper and two thick drawing pencils on my bed. As far as I knew, Cousin Abigail didn't tell Papa about my drawing either. I was grateful for that and for her silence about my lavish use of candles.

Dear Joseph,

    I'm up early, pinched awake by the throbbing muscles of my arms and legs. I sat on my bed a while, rubbing the sorest places, discouraged and disgusted. It seems no matter how often I have escaped the domestic drudgery sanctioned for women of my time, I am returned to it again and again. At St. Mary's Haven, I am obliged, strained as I am by the weight of my belly and overall ill-health of carrying a child, to do physical labor to help earn my keep and show I am suitable for employment after I leave. Many wealthy ladies of Michigan Avenue are sympathetic to our plight, Mother Superior tells us, and stand ready to employ us as domestic servants.

    Worst of all is the heavy, miserable work we do in the laundry room adjoining the kitchen. Several hours a week we wash linen and clothes – the nuns', Father Gerald's, our own, or that of some parishioners of St. Mary's Cathedral. Yesterday, my station was with two other girls over a large tub of hot water, rubbing lye soap into dirty clothes. I sometimes think of Sally, who no doubt continues to do the same in Shoreside for Cousin Abigail. Some girls rinse and wring out garments at another tub, while others must go out in the winter wind and cold to pin them to lines that crisscross the yard. When the laundry is frozen dry, it is carried into the kitchen for pressing. The two irons we use must be continuously reheated on the cook stove until the room is as hot as a blacksmith's forge. We alternately perspire and shiver through the process. Our hands redden and swell and crack from the constant water and harsh soap. We complain, some a little, some a lot, but not for the ears of the sisters, and especially not Mother Superior.

    I have been both grateful to and wary of Mother Superior since that brutal winter morning last month she accepted me, nauseous and utterly wretched, into the home. A tall, angular woman with arched eyebrows, she talks in a confident, blustery way reminiscent of Cousin Sherman but with a lilt to her speech that sounds foreign. Regally seated at a large roll top desk in her upstairs office/sitting room, she asked her keen-eyed questions, including "and how did you come to be pregnant, my dear?" I had made up a story (at my boarding house, a traveling salesman, overcome with lust, broke into my room) which she recorded along with my other answers on a fresh page in a large ledger. Relieved she seemed to accept this lie, I quickly agreed to doing my share of domestic work and having my mail read, another woman as chaperone on any excursion outside the home, and only female visitors. I would also attend a daily prayer service and, even if not a practicing Catholic, listen to Father Gerald say Sunday Mass in the parlor. I told one other lie in our meeting, that a friend had told me of St. Mary's Haven rather than the truth, that I had learned of it when I lived not far from here at Jacob Hoffman's mansion. (That's another part of my life I may as well reveal, the humiliation of my life with him paling in comparison with my present situation.) From my studio window on the third floor of Jacob's house I sometimes gazed at the imposing spire of St. Mary's Cathedral, which stands some blocks south, thinking of the modest one of St. Catherine's in Shoreside. Then, one day, I passed by here and read the small sign, St. Mary's Haven, over the front door.

When I returned to Jacob's, I asked the maid Caroline if the large brick house in the middle of Madison Street was a convent. Caroline's family had lived in the neighborhood for many years, and she knew nearly everything about its residents.

"That's the place where the sisters take care of women until their time comes," she answered airily.

"What time?"

"To have their babies, Miss."

"Oh."

Caroline gave me a sly look and added, "They take only girls who are otherwise respectable and have been betrayed."

Disturbed by this but preoccupied with other worries, I put the incident out of my mind until desperation called forth memory of the home and I made my way as a supplicant to its door.

Of course, I am not a model prisoner or "fallen woman," as Sister Margaret refers to us. From the beginning, I have sneaked out for solitary walks. One way or another I will keep the reply to my letter from Mother Superior's eyes. Female-only visitors is a rule I don't break since I don't have visitors, male or female. As for religion, I grit my teeth at the subjection to Catholic devotions.

Later, and now much excited! ... After the evening prayer service in the parlor, Elise stopped me in the front hall.

"Your last name is Willoughby, Victoria?"

"Yes." I was pleased by her friendly overture.

"You're a painter?"

I was too surprised to stop the nodding of my head. "I thought I was right!" Her cheeks flushed. "You painted my mother's portrait. Mrs. Thomasina Farnsworth."

I recognized the name and now recalled her mother, totally unlike her daughter except for black hair. Her features were so ordinary I had struggled to give her likeness a spark of individuality.

"Mother used to say you had such a stare, looking back and forth between her face and the canvas. You never seemed to blink. And you still have it. The stare, I mean."

"I do? I didn't know that."

Elise went on, "She also thought it quite strange you did not wear a bustle."

"It got in my way moving around the studio," I said. We both laughed. "How did you connect me with the painting, may I ask?"

"You signed it, of course, and it hangs in our drawing room."

After a moment, I said, "How is your mother?"

Elise's eyes filled with tears. "Mother died last year."

"I'm so sorry."

She hesitated. "Your beautiful painting of her has been a comfort."

"You still have it." I had little memory of the portraits I had done in Jacob's house once their owners had carried them away. I did care about doing my best to paint a fair representation of the person before me, but the image did not live in my memory.

"Of course."

There was a pause.

"When this is over, you will resume painting?" Elise asked.

"I don't know." I had drawn the bracelet but could I go on being an artist now that I was once again poor? I had accepted Jacob's money and lust in order to be a painter. When I ran away from his rage, I left behind the means to continue the artist's life. After I left St. Mary's Haven, I would be back in the same situation I'd always been in – needing money to live. Did I have the heart for it once my daughter was born and had gone to the home I wanted for her?

I hadn't known the length of my silence until Elise said, "Are you all right, Victoria?"

I tried to smile. "Yes, please forgive me. My brain is in a muddle these days, and the words I think I speak are not heard out loud. What are your plans, Elise?"

"I have means and a dear elderly aunt and uncle in Philadelphia who know nothing of my plight. Now that I'm alone in the world, they've invited me to stay with them anytime. Actually, I've thought I'd like to pursue a profession – perhaps photography. It's fascinating, don't you think?"

"It is," I agreed. "When I was a girl, I once worked in a daguerreotype studio. The photographer was also my schoolteacher. He encouraged my art."

"How fortunate and interesting!" Elise exclaimed. "Did you ever have your picture taken?"

"Yes, by Mr. Briscoe, that photographer. A family picture."

"How I would love to learn to operate a camera!"

"I believe it's not as hard now that the process has become easier – and much cleaner. And I have heard of female photographers," I added, moved by her enthusiasm.

Elise stepped closer to me and put a slim hand on my shoulder. "I have an idea. Why don't you come to Philadelphia and teach me what you know about photography? It's a lovely city, and did you know there are art schools open to women there?"

I was silent, stunned by the tantalizing possibilities in her words.

She saw my face and smiled, patting my shoulder. "Well, please think about it and we'll talk again soon. I guess we should go to bed. Good night."

✳

...It's now very late, the dark wee hours of the next day. I still can't sleep and sit at my desk wrapped in a blanket. I dare not count on a rich girl's fancy that she could forget tomorrow! But Elise has given me hope, just as Mr. Briscoe has more than once. Dear Mr. Briscoe...

Daguerreotype
(Shoreside, April 1858)

❝An odd one, Mr. Briscoe," Cousin Sherman had remarked once at dinner. "A smart teacher, a clever man, but not one for company."

He added Mr. Briscoe was a bachelor and lived with his parents a short distance from school.

Mr. Briscoe and the other teacher, thin, long-nosed Mr. Cartwright, took turns supervising recess. When it was Mr. Briscoe's turn, he read at his desk while I sat drawing at mine. We worked in harmonious quiet, he lost in sighs and mumbles over one book or another, his face nearly touching the page, while I, similarly lost, bent over my paper.

One sour spring morning, I struggled to draw a scatter of gray clouds, raising my eyes to the sky outside the window and lowering them to my paper. With each stroke, I became more agitated by the constantly shifting shapes until I threw down my pencil and ripped the drawing in two.

"Victoria?" Mr. Briscoe called. "What are you doing?"

"It's no good, Sir," I replied, hearing my voice shake.

"Stop tearing it up, whatever it is, and bring it here, please," he commanded.

I was on my feet, down the aisle, and up on the platform beside his desk without stopping to think. I laid the two pieces before him. Close up, a sharp and unfamiliar chemical odor from his clothing stung my nose.

Gently, the teacher eased together the torn edges and studied my work. "So this is what you've been doing all these weeks when your classmates are out playing." He frowned up at me.

"Yes, Sir."

"This is *your* kind of play."

"Yes, Sir." I smiled, a bit comforted.

"What else do you like to draw besides the sky?"

"Anything I see, objects of any kind, Sir."

"Do you also draw people?"

"No, I don't know how, Sir." His question stirred up my frustration. "What is the use of trying that if I don't know how? I can't even draw clouds right, how can I do a person?"

I stopped abruptly, my thoughts racing on. *There's no artist in Shoreside to teach me and I have no money for lessons anyway.*

"You will learn someday," Mr. Briscoe said in his lecture voice. "I am sure of it."

"Yes, Sir."

He pointed to the dark-covered book he had set aside to look at my drawing. "Ever heard of a daguerreotype?"

"No, Sir." I read the title, *American Handbook of the Daguerreotype,* puzzling over the strangeness of the word. Something to do with swords?

"Well, Victoria, it's the most exciting invention you can imagine! A new way to make a copy of an object in our real world. But not by painting or drawing. A Frenchman named Louis Daguerre discovered it nearly twenty years ago."

"I don't understand, Sir."

"Look, the book that came in my kit explains." Mr. Briscoe flipped to a page with an illustration of some kind of box on a three-legged pole. "All you need is this camera, strong daylight, and some chemicals. Any man can learn the technique if he studies it and buys the equipment."

"How does it work?" My anger had slipped away.

Seemingly by memory, he turned to another page with more illustrations. "Ah, that's what I'm experimenting with now. Basically, you polish a silvered copper plate, coat it with iodine and bromide, and put it in the camera. When you reflect the light from the object in front of it, it makes an impression on the plate. You make the image permanent with a mercury vapor, and, *voila*, as Mr. Daguerre would say, you have the copy."

"Oh."

Mr. Briscoe laughed, mistaking my one word of wonder for incomprehension. "Well, it's not easy to understand unless you see it done. But, Victoria, I believe it's like being an artist, practicing over and over until you get a clear, good image of what you want."

"It doesn't come out right every time?"

"By no means." Mr. Briscoe closed the book. "By no means," he repeated, as the bell rang and the first students began returning to the classroom, staring curiously up at us. "But I intend to become a daguerreotype operator very soon, making images of people. And I hope the Willoughbys will bring you to my studio so you can see what I mean."

A few weeks later, there was no hesitation when Paul brought the hand-printed notice to his parents in the dining room. Cousin Abigail read it out loud. "*Mr. Briscoe's Daguerreotype Studio, 12 Sycamore Street. Be the first in Shoreside with a one-of-a-kind photograph preserved, under glass, in a lovely velvet-lined case. One dollar and up per picture. Three sizes available. Appointments available Saturdays until June, and six days a week in the summer.*"

She laid it on the sideboard. "Well, it's high time we had this service in Shoreside." Taking her place at the table, she waved us to our chairs. "Having a picture taken at a gallery on Broadway has been fashionable in New York for years," she said. "I hear all the famous politicians sit for a Mr. Matthew Brady."

"Well, in my position then, I shall sit for Mr. Henry Briscoe if I can't go to New York," Cousin Sherman replied. "We shall have one of the whole family, including little Victoria," he decided.

"As you wish, dear," Cousin Abigail said with a pursing of lips in my direction.

Nancy Hagen Patchen

The following Saturday the five of us – Cousin Sherman, Cousin Abigail, Michael, Paul and I – rode in a carriage to Mr. Briscoe's house at eleven in the morning, each of us in our most formal attire. Cousin Sherman and Michael sported their best wool coats, waistcoats, and trousers in rich brown and deep blue, respectively. Paul's coat and trousers were tan; he was too young for a waistcoat, which he didn't mind, the more comfortable clothes the better for him. I wore my red velvet Sunday dress and Mama's bracelet, which I never took off. Cousin Abigail appeared in a close-fitting violet silk flounced dress and matching velvet shoes. She was flushed from lack of air, having instructed Sally to pull her corset strings as tight as possible. Both of us had our hair tied at the back of our heads, hers in loops, mine in braids.

Mr. Briscoe met us at the door and led us, apologizing for the climb to the top floor. "The strongest light is up here and I need the maximum for the best pictures," he said.

The studio was a square room with a skylight cut into the roof. On one side I recognized the camera, a black cloth draped over it, and a tripod from the illustration in Mr. Briscoe's book. He ushered us to a row of chairs and a round table with a plant and leather-bound book against the opposite wall. Behind the table hung a dark maroon panel. "Please sit down and excuse me for a moment," he said.

The air smelled of Mr. Briscoe's clothing at school. The odor grew stronger as he crossed the room, opened the door of an adjoining room, and went in. He came out again with some silvered plates in his hand and closed the door. He placed them on a table next to the camera.

"Please get ready to be still for thirty seconds at a time," he said, pushing the table out of the way.

Cousin Sherman smoothed his bushy side whiskers and cleared his throat as if he were going to make a speech. "Don't worry, this stiff collar won't let me," he joked. He certainly didn't look like himself in a sober pose, though it suited Cousin Abigail well. Her only difficulty was gasping for breath, which Mr. Briscoe warned might make the image blurry.

Cousin Sherman and Cousin Abigail sat side by side with Michael, Paul and me standing behind them. Mr. Briscoe gave me a box to stand on because I was so short. For the next hour, we posed in respectful silence while across the room Mr. Briscoe muttered, putting in and taking out plates, tossing the cloth over and off his head, peering through the lens and reminding us not to move.

71

When the finished picture was delivered in a gilt frame and velvet case, Cousin Sherman and Cousin Abigail were delighted. "The mirror tells me what I look like," Michael said with a wink. "I bet there are daguerreotype operators on every block of cities like Chicago and St. Louis," Paul said. I was silent, stunned by the way our likenesses had been captured, not by a mirror, not by a painter, but by a machine and light.

A few days later at school, Mr. Briscoe said, "If my business grows, I'll need an assistant to do some hand coloring and help me clean plates and take care of the equipment. I had thought of asking one of the boys, but since you are already an artist, Victoria" – here he grinned – "I thought perhaps you would like to help me."

This time I didn't hold back. "More than anything in the world," I said, forgetting to call him Sir.

Entry 12 -- 10 Mar. 1868 – Weather: Rainy in a.m., clearing in p.m.

Dear Joseph,

This morning, after a vivid dream of working at my easel, I had a waking vision of the girls of St. Mary's Haven as stormy images on a canvas, swirling gray clouds of repentance, darkened with black streaks of boredom and fatigue. Most of them, I think, want only to be forgiven, not reformed, and freed to resume their pre-Haven life (in my imagination, a feverish yellow-orange miasma over the dark clouds). Around the sewing table and over the washtubs, they tell their stories, which seem no less appalling than my own might be to them were I to tell it.

For example, the pock-faced girl, Jane, with a bosom that protrudes nearly as much as her stomach, plans to return as nanny to the three children of the newly widowed father who impregnated her, as soon as she gives away his latest child, his fourth, her first. "Mr. Julian says we'll marry in a few years, when the proper mourning period for his wife has been respected," Jane says, her finger worrying an indented pox scar above her lip.

Her feisty, petite roommate, Alice, holds a similar view. A maid seduced by the wealthy head of another household, Alice can not return there because the wife knows of the liaison. "He's waiting for me to get out. He loves me," she insists, chin up, looking us in the eye.

Another girl, Elizabeth, works at the county hospital. She is so thin she looks like a pole with a balloon attached to its middle. A well-known Catholic doctor drugged her drink as they took refreshment after a long night shift. Afterward, he made all the arrangements for her to enter St. Mary's Haven and sent additional donations to the home. "He cares about me," she insists, crossing ropey arms over a distended stomach. "I can go back to my work, on a different floor."

Sarah and Emma, who occupy the room next to mine, are stupid shop girls with pretty faces and bad teeth who smell of the vanilla they use as makeshift perfume. They have illusions not of marriage but of romance. After dinner, I hear their excited voices reading aloud lurid excerpts from magazine stories. These are the same women who go up to the sisters after prayers and with lowered eyes and dribbling tears lament their sad fate. But when the sisters are out of earshot, one or the other confides, "I can't wait to get out of this place. There are plenty of men who'd enjoy my company."

The truly pitiable one among us is Jean, a narrow-jawed factory worker who can't read or write and often reeks of body odor despite the sisters' efforts to encourage cleanliness. She wanders around with an anxious smile, meekly agreeing to whatever is said. Sarah and Emma delight in telling her outlandish stories, such as there are sea serpents in Lake Michigan or the South really won the War, to see her eager nods. Her dismal helplessness drags me out of my own misery long enough to sit next to her at meals when no one else will. (Sister Margaret smiles at me when I do so, and I notice she holds her biting tongue with the girl.) That some man, probably the first one who pretended he found Jean attractive, backed her against a wall and forced his way between her limp flanks is no surprise. She has no expectations of men but would like to keep her baby. While the rest of us are frightened of childbirth, Jean talks only of the baby's arrival. "I'll have someone to love and to love me," she says to me over and over."

Of course, that's what all women crave, one way or another, suspending themselves in the soothing waters of love. I have been more like a shore rock under a blazing sun that the waves rarely reach with blessed coolness. The loveliest wave was you, Joseph, and now the rock once again, and forever, stands dry and alone.

I can not bear yet to write of you....

Here I forced my thoughts back to Paul. Knowing him made all the difference in what I have become. Though the bell has rung for breakfast and my stomach is hollow, I must tell this part of the story.

First Kiss
(Shoreside, 1859)

In early September of 1859, I returned to the Willoughby's house from a miserable summer with Papa for my final school term, eighth grade. I was thirteen and Paul fourteen. He had graduated the May before and was working at Willie's to learn the business as Michael had. In the three months we'd been apart, Paul had grown taller and his angular freckled face had lost its boyish look.

After dinner that first night, still giddy over my escape from the island, I agreed to go with Paul to visit Sandy. I kept my distance while he fed her an apple and slapped on her saddle. But I found myself running after him when he climbed on and said, "C'mon, Victoria. I'm going to ride Sandy and then let her roll on the sand." An hour later, breathless and laughing from romping up and down the beach, we returned Sandy to the stable. Paul brushed her down, and I filled her bucket with water from the well.

We were still in high spirits as we walked toward the house. I picked up a stick and waved it at Paul. He found another stick and we mock-battled to the well and around it, then on to duck under the clothesline strung between poles and dash around the privy, snorting and holding our noses. When we tired of our game, we flopped on the grass beneath the birch tree along the back fence to share a dipper of water. A light breeze tickled the pale green leaves of the low branches against our faces. I straightened my skirt and saw a rip near the hem. I was thinking that I'd try to mend it before Cousin Abigail noticed when Paul said, as quietly as I'd ever heard him speak, "As soon as the War starts, Victoria, I'm joining the Union Army."

"Oh, Paul, no!" I grabbed his arm and felt the tensed muscle under the rough sleeve. "You're not even near sixteen!"

"Less than two years. And I can probably add a year on when I sign up." He gave me the same smile he used with his mother.

"That's wrong, you shouldn't do that," I protested.

He grinned. "Why, wouldn't you be proud if your second cousin went off to war and fought for the liberty of Indiana?"

I leapt up like he'd hit me with his stick. "No, I wouldn't. You mustn't let anything happen to you," meaning, we both knew, get killed.

Paul's smile disappeared. Instantly, he unfolded his long legs and scrambled to his feet beside me. Blindly, I threw my arms around him and cried into his chest.

"Oh, sweetheart," he said. I shivered at the sudden endearment. The next thing I knew, he had pulled back and lowered his head to kiss me full on the mouth, his lips smooth and warm. After that kiss came another and another. When I finally opened my eyes, I saw in the night sky above us the dazzle of the North Star, which I often wished I could reach up and touch. I had once sat at my bedroom window and drawn it, but how much more beautiful it was outdoors, the light a glorious sparkling whiteness like shards of ice.

Victoria's Quest

In my confusion of thought and emotion, the figure in a long pale gown billowing toward us across the lawn looked like the ghost of the lighthouse. It was no apparition, but Cousin Abigail.

"What is going on here?" she demanded.

"Oh, is it time to go in, Mother?" Paul said. "Victoria and I were talking about what we did over the summer."

Cousin Abigail glared at him. "Victoria was acting most improperly with you." She turned to me. "Just like your mother. I knew it."

I put on my blank look and said nothing, though I was fuming inside. *Why did Cousin Abigail have to compare me to Mama when I had nothing to do with what happened?*

"Honestly, Mother, we were just talking." Paul stepped close to her, smiling and touching her shoulder.

Cousin Abigail hesitated only a moment. "Well, it didn't look like talking, whatever it was. And the responsibility for conduct is Victoria's. She can not act this way and be allowed to stay under our roof." She swung around, her petticoat like a whirling top, and we followed her into the house.

Shortly thereafter, while Paul and I each kept to our rooms, we could hear her carrying on downstairs in the parlor, not her words but her voice, except once when she raised it to nearly a shout: "They're second cousins but she is simply not good enough for my son." I doubt it would have made any difference for Paul to stand up for me, but I felt ashamed when he didn't. But Cousin Sherman answered nearly as loudly in my defense, and that has always counted for much in my feeling for him.

"Now, now, she's all right, my dear. Give her a second chance. She means no harm. We can afford some Christian charity." In the end, he managed to persuade her that I could stay and that he would speak to Papa about it, who would certainly make sure it didn't happen again.

"She's too independent for her own or anyone's good." Cousin Abigail had the last word. I understood then that her unhappiness about her life in Shoreside, whatever dreams she gave up for marriage and children, was taken out on servants, tradesmen, and me. In spite of supplying me with drawing paper and pencils, she could not accept my refusal to show true humility, as they did, in her presence.

In the next weeks, my rush of feelings for Paul unleashed a firestorm in my head, as I went to sleep at night. I was joyful, yes, to know Paul cared for me as I had come to care for him. Still, while the troubling spirit of the lighthouse had not visited me in the Willoughby house, I felt the same torment of fear that something invisible was poised to take my happiness away when I least expected it. These were the first of my nameless fears, the ones that have caused me the most pain over the past years. I could tell no one of these strange mind states, especially Paul. He would not know what I was talking about, he who met each day clear-eyed and optimistic.

Amid the chaos of my feelings was a return of thoughts about my mother, questions I had been too angry to think about after I had gotten her letter. For the first time, I tried to picture what had happened after she left us that day in Shoreside. How had she gotten to Chicago? She could have taken a horse, I supposed, though the distance between Shoreside and Chicago must be a hundred miles. Could she have traveled that far on horseback? Maybe she rode in a wagon headed that way instead. Or on the train? Did she go alone? Her only real friend was Maggie Fogarty, and Maggie never left Shoreside. As far as I knew, Mama had no money, and she would have needed some, no matter how she traveled to Chicago. She must have borrowed the money from someone. But who?

Putting that question aside as unanswerable for now, I conjured up a reunion with Mama in a vague future when she had gotten rich in her new life. I couldn't picture exactly how, but I knew it would have to do with music and her gay charm, entertaining people in Chicago. She'd come back to Shoreside and find me at the Willoughbys. Dressed in the latest fashion, far more elegant than Cousin Abigail's attire, she would announce, "I've come to take Victoria with me to Chicago where we will live our lives as true ladies." Somewhere in Chicago, wherever she lived, we would spend happy hours filling in stories of what we have each done since she'd left. As soon as I heard the explanation of the lost years from her lips, I would understand and forgive. We would make plans for our future, strolling the fine streets of the city, looking in store windows, stopping for an afternoon pastry and tea in a hotel dining room – laughing now and then at that quaint life we had led on the island. Buoyed by these fantasies, I tried several times to draw a picture of Mama's face. I could sketch only her soft curls around a blank oval.

Only later did I wonder why Paul was not a part of any of my imaginings.

Entry 13 - - 11 Mar. 1868 — Weather: Cool, sunny

Dear Joseph,

We're all in our seventh or eighth month, as far as we can tell. Jean has gained the most weight, her face puffy and her body mountainous, and has known with the least certainty when her pregnancy began. Yesterday, she came out of her room in the middle of the day holding her stomach and crying, "Help! Help! It hurts, I can't breathe!" Elizabeth went for Sister Margaret while Alice and I tried to hold Jean up. Sister Margaret arrived and, like Father Gerald on Sundays announcing the gospel, intoned, "Contractions have begun."

With us ringed around the staircase like mesmerized onlookers at a burning house, she helped Jean up to the second floor room used for deliveries. Mother Superior had pointed it out as I was moving in. I remembered it as no different from ours except for an extra table with a stack of linens. All afternoon as we quietly moved about and passed the stairs, we heard Jean's groans and cries. As evening began, they became louder and longer. At dinner, Elizabeth made the sign of the cross between bites of ham loaf. Jane put her hands over her ears and stared at her plate. Sarah and Emma rolled their eyes and sighed. Alice declared, "It won't be that bad for me." Elise got up in the middle of the meal and left the room. After a while, I went to another part of my mind and didn't hear a sound.

Jean's cries finally stopped after midnight, replaced by an echoing cry of a baby.

At breakfast, Sister Margaret told us, "Jean was a brave girl and will be fine. Her son was born healthy." She excused us from our morning's work, knowing none of us had slept the night before. She looked worn and oddly triumphant.

I couldn't go back to sleep and tried to sketch the scene out the window above my desk, as I used to in my attic room at Cousin Sherman's. It wasn't much of a view, only the dull brown side of the house next door. But it calmed me a bit to keep my hand busy as my mind raced. *What will my time be like?*

Victoria's Quest

Will I be brave? I hated the idea of being helpless before Sister Margaret and Mother Superior, at their mercy in my pain. I've had some bleeding I kept to myself, washing out the evidence in my room. *Will I contract childbed fever? Will I die? Oh, I must first bring my daughter into the world!*

My thoughts wandered on as I decided to make my window and its yellowed muslin curtains part of the drawing. Why, if lovemaking is a pleasure, must childbirth cause so much pain? Still, what female thinks of pain when she falls in love, especially for the first time? Tonight, after napping fitfully this afternoon, I decided to set down more of those eventful months with Paul during which Sadie (who, it occurs to me, would willingly accept the dangers of childbirth) arrived at the Fogartys.

Sadie
(Shoreside, Fall 1859)

At the Willoughbys, Paul and I avoided each other, including even glances at the dinner table. Still, I don't know why Cousin Abigail thought the romance was over as long as we could walk home from school together. It was not hard to sneak behind a fence or a tree along the path to kiss and hug. Soon, Paul had made a plan for our future. "We'll get married in three years. You'll be sixteen and legal and I should be out of the army. Father figures the war will be short. You can help Cousin Edward until I get back." As afraid as I was for him, I understood his eagerness to join the army, with its opportunity to see the world outside Shoreside as he always longed to do. "A man gets good pay in the army, I hear. Enough for us to start married life if Mother and Father are opposed to our marrying." Paul grinned.

"That seems so far away, three years," I said. I accepted his vision of the future while not being able to imagine it coming to pass. Life with his sunny optimism should put an end to my dark moods as well as my impossible dream of being an artist. But, deep down, I didn't believe it.

Meanwhile, I liked going to school, mainly because of Mr. Briscoe. For my lunchtime drawing, he loaned me his books on art and gave me extra paper and pencil from his personal supply. What Cousin Abigail had given me was long gone and now I dared not ask her for more. True to his promise, Mr. Briscoe hired me, for twenty cents a day, to work at his studio every Saturday until winter darkness set in. I saved every penny for more paper and pencils except once when I bought two ribbons for my hair – one yellow, one blue – to wear to school. I had several tasks, all exciting. I polished and buffed the silver plates on the copper sheets. Mr.

Briscoe exposed them in the darkroom to an iodine vapor, the source of that smell in the studio that now clung to my clothes as well as his. This vapor, I learned, made the plates sensitive to light for the camera. I also helped arrange props and chairs and showed people how to assume the poses Mr. Briscoe decided took best advantage of the light and the features of their faces. Best of all, between appointments, I sat in a curtained alcove of the studio to put the finishing touches on the daguerreotypes. I used a brush and ink to fill in broken lines or smooth the image. Then I mounted each picture in a frame with a mat, backing, and gilt or black oak moldings and corners. "You have a natural talent, Victoria," he said more than once. I basked in his praise and his trusting me to choose the frame, if the customer had not specified one. Pretending they were portraits drawn by my own hand, I inscribed a tiny V.W. on the back of each one.

On sunless Saturdays when Mr. Briscoe couldn't take pictures, I usually found a way to go to the Fogartys. Sometimes, the morning train to Chicago rumbled by as I arrived at their house. I strained to see the faces in the passenger cars though there was no one I could possibly know.

I recall the constants of those Saturdays at the Fogarty house as soup bubbling on the stove and bread baking, children squabbling and laughing, Uncle Frank dragging in from his half-day at the mill, and Aunt Maggie hanging a quilt out an upstairs window, no matter the weather. She always seemed to be piecing together a quilt. She'd already made smaller ones for the children and a special one for her and Frank's bed in what she called an Irish Chain design.

I carried paper and pencil with me now, and after a cup of tea at the kitchen table, I often sketched a detail of the children's faces – Patricia's pout, Bridget's knobby nose, Peter's impish grin, and Sean's big ears. My favorite subject was baby Anna, who had wise, deep-set violet eyes with feathery blond lashes. I was getting the idea of expression, of how to capture a curve or line that revealed personality.

Aunt Maggie admired my sketches of the children but wouldn't stop rushing around herself long enough for me to do more than a scribbled impression of her face – plump cheeks and stubborn chin, damp wisps of hair on her temples escaping from her tight bun, and snapping blue eyes.

One Saturday, I did my first drawing of a whole person – Uncle Frank sitting at the kitchen table. He was the only Fogarty who stayed in one place in the house for any length of time. He was smoking a cigarette and reading the newspaper to Aunt Maggie. "I don't have the time to read," she said to me, as he folded back a page and she kneaded bread dough across the table from him. I wondered if she could read, having watched her sound out letters on signs and labels. The most interesting article Uncle Frank read aloud was an account of a skirmish of Union and Confederate soldiers that had taken place some weeks before. Listening and drawing, I was thinking about Paul and hoping the fighting would cease before it became a full-blown war. As if hearing my fear, Uncle Frank said, "I'm an able-bodied man, Maggie. I should join the local militia if it starts up." Aunt Maggie stopped punching the dough and glared at him, floury hands on hips. "You can't go, Frank. You have a family to support." Relief flitted across Uncle Frank's face, and then a faint longing, but he didn't argue. He was quiet like Papa, but an amiable kind of quiet, not a tense one like a powder keg about to explode. I tried to capture his calmness in my drawing but he said he looked like Simple Simon. I laughed along with everyone else.

One dark and cold Saturday in November, I found Aunt Maggie in the back yard, investigating why the chickens were squawking. We watched as a little Negro girl, with enormous eyes in a skinny face and as scrawny as an old hen herself, crawled out of the coop.

This was how I discovered the astonishing fact that Aunt Maggie and Uncle Frank Fogarty sometimes harbored runaway slaves from the South. "We don't tell anyone unless we have to, Victoria," Aunt Maggie said as the girl clung to a small cotton bag and quivered from head to toe. "The fewer people who know we're in the Underground Railroad, the safer it is for the Negroes. Have you ever noticed the quilt I hang out the window always has a yellow square in the center? That means this is a safe house."

While I gaped at these revelations, she stepped to the girl's side and put an arm around her bony shoulders. "Now, why didn't you just knock on the back door, little girl?" she asked.

"I'm scared, Missus." The girl's voice was barely above a whisper.

"Well, you're all right now." Aunt Maggie hugged her closer. "What's your name and how old are you?"

"My name's Sadie and I believe I am ten or eleven, Missus." The girl's eyes pooled with tears.

Aunt Maggie shook her head. "Well, it's time to get you out of sight, Sadie."

The girl didn't stop shaking even after Aunt Maggie brought her into the warm kitchen and sat her at the table with a large bowl of cabbage soup and a plate of sliced fresh bread. The Fogarty children crowded around her asking questions, but Uncle Frank shooed everyone out but Patricia, the oldest, and me. "Let the poor girl eat and then she can tell us about her journey," he said.

"Thank you, Suh," Sadie whispered. After the first spoonful, she did not slow her eating until every bite of soup and bread was gone.

"Now, a bath is the next thing for you," Aunt Maggie declared. She had Patricia and me pull the washtub close to the stove. We took turns filling it with buckets of water to which she added kettles full of heated water. We helped Sadie off with her raggedy dress and into the water. Naked, she began shivering again. She had chigger bites and cuts on her arms and legs and kept her eyes closed, moaning, as we gently washed the dirt from her sore skin. Afterwards, Aunt Maggie wrapped her in an old soft quilt. Her eyes drooping, Sadie smiled as the younger Fogartys returned to the kitchen.

"So, tell us where you're from," asked Peter, who had his mother's directness.

"Georgia. A plantation," Sadie said shyly. "Things were going bad and the master was all the time beating us." The Fogartys made various noises of anger while a chill tingled up and down my spine.

"What about your Mama and Daddy?" Aunt Maggie asked.

"Mama died when I was born, Missus. Daddy and I were going to come North together. He figured out a map. We got family near Chicago and Daddy was afraid the master was going to sell us to someone even worse any day." She untied the sack and handed a piece of paper to Aunt Maggie, who handed it to Uncle Frank. "This is the address Daddy had someone write down."

"So why are you alone?" Peter asked.

"Daddy got sick. He made me go without him." She hesitated. "Am I in Illinois now?"

We all laughed a little. "Not quite yet," Uncle Frank said softly. "But you're close. This is Indiana."

"Did anyone chase you?" asked Bridget, who moved quick as lightning like her mother.

"I don't know. I hurried and hurried and followed the North Star and Daddy's map. I slept in the woods and stole eggs from farms. I spied safe houses sometimes. They took me to the next town. That's how I got to Shoreside." Her voice faded with each sentence.

"Sadie is worn out," Aunt Maggie said briskly. "Let's put her up in the girls' bedroom to rest."

But it was impossible for the Fogartys to be quiet, and a few hours later Sadie was back downstairs, sleepy-eyed and eager for company. I was fascinated by her finely angled face and her brown skin, dark and richly silky in contrast to what seemed our coarse white pastiness. "I think you must be the princess granddaughter of a famous African king," I told her.

"Am I?" She seemed unsure whether or not to agree.

Before I left, sworn to secrecy about the Underground Railroad, I drew a sketch of Sadie, my emotion over her plight somehow impelling me to exaggerate the size of her eyes and thinness of her arms and legs.

"Is this what a princess looks like?" she said, turning down her mouth.

"Yes, that quilt is your long royal robe," I assured her.

Her pout turned into a bright smile when I gave her the sketch and said, "This is yours. A gift."

Entry 14 -- 13 Mar. 1868 – Weather: Blustery, cold

Dear Joseph,

My spirits had risen over the past few days, only to plummet in witnessing Jean's misery. Yesterday, up the stairwell, we heard her crying and begging, "He's my baby, I love him, he's all I'll ever have in this world, please, please!" and Sister Margaret's firm, "It's God's will," followed by Mother Superior's stentorian, "Now, dear, you know you are not very clever and not very strong and have no family to help. It's all for the best." I know it is the sisters' will, not God's, to take away Jean's son and give him up to adoption by Catholic parents. This morning, Jean returned to her room downstairs with us, her spirit, if not her mind, broken. She remained in bed, weeping, most of the day. Then, avoiding our eyes at dinner, she barely picked at the watery cod and murky Brussels sprouts, distractedly pressing a hand to her breasts, swollen with unused milk.

The wind blows angrily outside, and I think what price in sorrow we pay for a roof over our heads. How can any of us make sense of it – what we want, what we must do, what we can have or not have, according to society's rules? The hard reality of being a woman is so clear in my having to give birth to a child. I had been so sure there would be no consequences when you and I joined our bodies in love. There had been none before – either from my quick couplings with Paul or the violent ones with Jacob.

It's what I have found the hardest to accept about St. Mary's Haven – for Jean, the other women, and myself – not being in control of our fates, as I have tried through the years to be. And yet I must find a way to get my daughter to the best home for her.

Oh, will this wind ever stop adding its breath to the noise in my head?

Sin, pain, motherhood... consequences for what you do, Aunt Maggie liked to say, came straight from God to the sinner. "It's God's will" was her answer, too, to all questions, including why Anna coughed and ate little and ran constant fevers. When she accused Mama of sinning, it served only to spur me stubbornly toward my future.

Victoria's Quest

Lost and Found
(Shoreside, March 1860)

" The Catholic Church is where you belong, Victoria," Aunt Maggie announced that early spring Saturday while rain thrummed on the roof and the Fogarty children swirled around us. "If your mother had remained true to her faith..." She stopped to scold Bridget for nearly knocking over Anna, taking unsteady steps across the kitchen. I was startled: this was the first time she had spoken of Mama since her disappearance.

I hoisted frail Anna into my arms and smoothed the fine strands of her blond hair, anger stiffening my stroking hands as I took in Aunt Maggie's meaning.

Whether or not I belonged in the Catholic Church, I had been in St. Catherine's many times already. Paul had discovered the church was full of secret dim alcoves and always open. It was the perfect place for us to meet until school ended and I went back to the lighthouse for the summer. When we first began meeting here, I imagined Mama, crowded into one long pew with her sisters and brothers for Mass, as the Fogartys did now. I felt guilty about using the church for our romance, though I felt no presence of God, either approving or disapproving, as I felt none praying as Papa had insisted I do at bedtime.

Only last Thursday, on my fourteenth birthday, Paul and I had spent nearly an hour in St. Catherine's.

"I love you. Tell me you love me," he demanded, as he often did.

"I do, I do."

We pressed our bodies together, I kissing his face in a fever, he moving his hands over my breasts and buttocks as the flickering votives shadowed our bodies. "Only two more years, Victoria, and we'll always be together," he breathed.

Remembering those words, I found myself saying, "Oh, Aunt Maggie, I don't want to go back to the island."

"You must," she said loudly. "It's your duty to help your father." Then she turned and gazed out the water-streaked window. Her voice softened. "She had a mind of her own, Kathleen did – always getting into trouble."

"Like what?" I asked, feeling the heat of Anna's tiny body warming my chest.

Aunt Maggie pursed her lips. "Oh, she'd decide to jump out of the barn window with her eyes closed onto the haystack, or take all her clothes off on a hot summer's day to swim in the creek, or hitch a ride from a passing wagon into town – anything that was different and daring and away from the farm." Aunt Maggie smiled and shook her head. "Everyone else – me, included – followed her lead."

"Like the Pied Piper."

"And we were the rats?" Aunt Maggie gave me a mock frown and we both laughed.

"Kathleen didn't have a flute or pipe or whatever it was the Pied Piper had but she did love music, playing the piano, and dancing at the Tavistock," Aunt Maggie went on. "My, the times we had with the likes of Bill O'Leary and Peter Burgess and Dennis Flanagan."

I started at the last name. Anna reared her head to look at me. "Dennis Flanagan? Papa rescued him from the lake. He stayed overnight on the island. He and Mama laughed and sang songs." I remembered my blushing when he gave me a penny.

"Yes, that was Dennis, like Kathleen, always ready for a good time," Aunt Maggie agreed. "A bit of a dreamer. Said he wasn't going to spend his whole life tied down on the farm."

"Did he?" I kissed Anna's cheek. She nestled her head into my neck.

"His folks needed him so I hope he's done the right thing and stayed." Aunt Maggie paused and looked at me, and in the next breath, blurted, "Victoria, I love her but your mother has sinned greatly."

Giving her my blank look, I set Anna down gently on the floor and walked away thinking, *Mama left to follow not God's will but her own. I will, too...*

Sadie stayed three weeks before continuing on the journey to her family near Chicago. Every Saturday, I went to the Fogartys after I'd finished my work for Mr. Briscoe. Sadie had to stay in the house while the Fogarty children ran in and out of the house all day long. She sat shyly in the kitchen with Maggie until one of them came in to talk to her or ask her to play. Like me, she loved Anna and would hold her for hours.

Victoria's Quest

I braided her hair and taught her how to write her name on a piece of my drawing paper.

The following Saturday started out bright, but in the forenoon the sun disappeared under clouds and Mr. Briscoe let me go very early. After a year, the clamor of townspeople for a daguerreotype had quieted. There had been no scheduled sittings that morning.

When I came into the Fogarty kitchen, Uncle Frank told me, "You're just in time to say goodbye, Victoria. Someone at the flour mill is on his way." He took a sip of tea. "He's driving a wagon with a false bottom to hide Sadie. He'll go to Rodmell twenty-five miles west and deliver the flour to a warehouse and her to another safe house." He cleared his throat. This was a long speech for him.

I had learned that the Fogartys joined the Underground Railroad because of the new priest at St. Catherine's. Father Michael was brought from a very poor parish in West Virginia to take over for elderly Father Tom, who retired from ill health. Father Michael fiercely identified the plight of enslaved Negroes with that of his fellow Irish on two accounts – the cruel indifference of the English politicians to the Irish during the potato famine that drove them to America in the first place, and then their exploitation in America in the coal mines, which he had seen first hand. He had recruited safe houses among St. Catherine families, one by one. "Frank surprised me, how strong he felt," Aunt Maggie said. "I was willing to help the poor things, but he got worked up like I've never seen him."

By Uncle Frank's side now, Sadie stood teary-eyed, looking like a little brown clown layered in cast-off shirts and skirts and pants of all colors and sizes. But how much stronger and brighter she looked from my first sight of her crawling out of the chicken coop weeks earlier. On the table, Aunt Maggie was stuffing a cotton sack to bursting with biscuits, cheese, and apples.

"Oh, I'm going to miss you, Sadie!" I sat down and drew a quick sketch, which replaced her frown with a wide smile. I rolled up the paper and tucked it in her sack. "Something to look at until you get home." I patted her arm.

"So, don't cry," Bridget said. "You'll be with your own family soon."

"I maybe won't have anyone nice to play with, though, like I do here." Sadie stared down at the too-large pair of cracked shoes several Fogarty children had worn before her.

"You'll be fine." Aunt Maggie tied the strings of the sack. "We'll pray for you every night. You must trust in the Lord to provide for and protect you."

"Yes, Missus."

Giving Sadie a hug, I thought, *There's the Lord to trust and men to fear. What if someone is angry enough to follow one small slave girl? What if she is captured outside Shoreside and taken back to her life of misery in the South?*

The rumble of horses' hooves and creaking of wagon wheels stopped in front of the house. Uncle Frank stood up. "Roger is here." He opened the door to a short, wiry man.

"Good afternoon, Frank. Is she ready?" the man said at once.

In the next minute, Sadie had crawled with her sack into the space at the bottom of the wagon, cushioned by one of Aunt Maggie's quilts. Sacks of floor were rearranged on top, and Roger drove off. No one dared call out a final goodbye.

Later, not eager to return to the Willoughbys, I decided to go a few streets out of my way back to Front Street. I came to the noisy, smelly livery stable on Fifth Street full of restless, pawing horses and rough men. I hurried past and turned into the next street, one I had never been on, lined with small dark workshops. Feeling uneasy, I was turning around at the blacksmith's shop when I saw a sign in the window in the office next to it. *Campbell's Detective Agency, J.J. Rankin, agent,* it said. Cousin Sherman had said once at dinner that railroad companies were hiring detectives to prevent thefts of money and mail on the trains. There was something about that name in the window. Suddenly, I felt I had to know more about J.J. Rankin.

Quickly, I opened the door and walked in. Two chairs flanked a table with a stack of railroad timetables and a copy of the weekly newspaper. A black, potbellied stove nearby pleasantly warmed the air. Behind it was a low partition. A man, seated at a desk working by lantern light, stood up immediately and came toward me. He was short and solid and wore a brown suit that seemed a bit small for his hefty stomach. He had a full head of dark red hair, parted down the middle, and a curled mustache that looked carefully maintained.

"May I help you, Miss?" His voice was deep and firm.

"You are a detective, Sir?"

"Yes, indeed. Mr.J.J. Rankin at your service."

It hit me. *The name in the lighthouse log. This is what Papa had left me alone on the island for – to ask the detective to find Mama!* I swallowed hard. "I'm Victoria Willoughby. I'm pleased to meet you."

He looked at me with interest. "Are you related to Sherman Willoughby, the railroad car maker?"

"Yes, he's my cousin – well, my father's cousin. Edward Willoughby."

He gave his own start of recognition. *So I was right!* "Please, come in and sit down." He opened the door and gestured to a chair in front of his desk. Behind him on the wall was a large map of states showing the railroad lines between Baltimore and St. Louis. Next to it stood a tall wood filing cabinet.

I sat quickly but only on the edge of the chair.

Waiting for my next words, Mr. Rankin neatened the papers on his already tidy desk.

I gathered my courage. "My father came to you about my mother."

He looked up. "Yes, I do recollect that."

"Well, Papa can't leave the lighthouse this time of year, and I'm boarding in town so he sent me to see if you've succeeded in finding her."

"Hmm." Mr. Rankin rubbed an eyelid with the back of a finger. "I'll see if I have a file."

He pulled an impressive ring of keys from a desk drawer. *What secret doors and boxes did they all open,* I wondered. When he stepped to the cabinet, I saw that his stomach protruded not from flesh, as I had first thought, but the concealed gun under his jacket. With surprising deftness, his stubby fingers unlocked the lower drawer, flipped through the folders, and plucked one out. "Yes, here it is." Back at his desk, he took his time reading the one-page report while I strained to make out the words upside down, which I couldn't.

He coughed. "There's a slight problem."

"You couldn't find Mama?" I blurted.

"Not that, no." He kept his eyes fixed on the report. "There's a balance due before I can release any information."

"Oh, of course," I said as if I had forgotten for a moment. "How much do we still owe?"

Mr. Rankin pursed his lips. "Fifteen dollars."

"I see." I tried to conceal my despair. *Fifteen dollars!* I had earned only a few dollars in all the time I had worked for Mr. Briscoe. It'd take forever to earn fifteen dollars. "Well, I'll come back later, then. Thank you."

"I'm here six days a week, in and out," Mr. Rankin said.

Entry 15 -- 16 Mar. 1868 – Weather: Fair, light breeze

Dear Joseph,
    This morning, I sat down at the breakfast table and held my breath a moment against the unpleasantly ashy smell of Sister Barbara's burned biscuits. Elizabeth said, "Jean's not here, and I have to tell you what happened last night." Used to the evening shift at the hospital, Elizabeth often wakes in the wee hours, thinking it's time to go on duty. Slowly, she dribbled milk into her bowl of oatmeal, then looked around the table to see that she had our attention.
    "So, tell us," Alice said, breaking off a charred biscuit top.
    "Well, it must have been after midnight." Elizabeth stirred gray-and-white spirals in her oatmeal. "As you know, my room is closest to the staircase. I heard someone come down the steps and say something, so I cracked open my door to look."
    "The sisters thought there was a burglar," Sarah said, grinning and rolling her eyes at Emma.
    "No!" Elizabeth stopped her spoon, and her words tumbled out. "There, at the foot of the stairs, Sister Margaret was handing Jean's baby, bundled like a white cocoon – it had to be hers, no one else has a baby yet – into someone's arms, I couldn't see who. At first I thought it was a woman, the person was so small. They didn't talk, but there were tears on Sister Margaret's face, and when the person turned to leave, I saw it was a man with a beard."
    When she finished, there was a heavy silence. We weren't prepared for this reality. My thoughts jumped haphazardly. *Where was the baby taken... Jean was not allowed to say goodbye... as if her son had never existed, as if she had carried nothing inside her body for nine months... Sister Margaret crying... No man other than Father Gerald and Doctor Stephens had set foot in this house, and then to come in and take the baby. Who was this man? My baby girl, who will be a surprise to all when she is seen for the first time...Will I know the bond between us has snapped the night she's taken away?*

93

Victoria's Quest

"Where do our babies go?" Emma asked loudly. Across the room, Sister Barbara jerked her head and frowned, interrupting the sipping of her tea. Taking a bite of biscuit, Alice sent her a friendly wave.

"Shhh," whispered Jane, whose forehead was a poppy field of fresh pimples. "We have to trust they will be placed in the very best loving home." The oatmeal in her bowl remained uneaten.

"Elizabeth, you'd better not tell Jean," Sarah said, pushing away from the table.

"Sister Margaret probably did already." Elizabeth put on her matter-of-fact nurse's tone.

As everyone left the dining room, Elise said, "I desperately need some fresh air, Victoria."

"I'll go with you. There are a few minutes before sewing class."

Outdoors, it was unseasonably mild for early spring. As we strolled up one side of the street and back the other, soft air moved across our faces. Around the houses, bushes and trees were beginning to sprout new green. A sweet cinnamon aroma of baking apple pie drifted from an open window, carrying me back to Rose's kitchen on Saturdays.

"Why was Sister Margaret crying?" I asked.

Elise shook her head, too consumed with asking her own question. "I wonder if I'll feel like Jean when my child is born."

"You mean, want to keep it?" I barely noticed the two snorting horses pulling a smart carriage past us.

"Yes, keep it despite the censure of society and," she added bitterly, "my hatred of its father."

"Hatred?" I was taken aback. One of the few emotions I do not feel is hate for my baby's father.

"Yes, hatred. I'll tell you one day soon." Then she stopped in mid-stride and gripped my hand. "But what am I talking about? A woman in my position can't live openly with a bastard child."

"And you're going to start a new life as a photographer," I reminded her.

"Yes, that's right," she said, brightening. "Have you decided to come with me?"

"I'd love to but I don't have the money," I managed to say.

"Don't be so sure," Elise said mysteriously as we went back inside St. Mary's Haven.

Later, as we returned to Sister Barbara's mercies for lunch, Sister Margaret limped to our table and announced with a broad smile. "Excuse me, girls. I've brought someone who'd like to meet you. This is my brother, Dennis Kelly. He teaches at St. Clare's School for Boys." Next to her, also smiling, stood a small man with a beard.

Elizabeth gasped.

Sister Margaret paused. "Are you all right, Elizabeth?"

"Fine, thank you, Sister. Sorry." Elizabeth busied herself arranging utensils next to her plate.

The rest of us knew at once this was the same man Elizabeth had seen last night, and I flushed, remembering his letter that I had intercepted and read. From that letter, somehow I had pictured a big man with rough good looks. The real Dennis Kelly was short, compact, and fine-featured. Whatever his appearance, if he was the man who placed the babies into homes, I must get on his good side!

Brother and sister sat down. Sister Margaret introduced us one by one. As we exchanged "Good Afternoons," he scanned each face like it was the first page of an interesting new book.

Now seeing an empty place, Sister Margaret said, "Jean is not here?"

"Nor at breakfast or sewing class, Sister," Jane reported.

Sister Margaret glanced at her brother and stood up. "I must check on her right away." She hobbled out the door.

"I hope she's all right," I said, as the others glanced uneasily at each other.

"I'm sure she's fine," Dennis said firmly.

We began to eat our vegetable stew. It was mushy and tasteless. Dennis seemed too full of questions to notice. In short order, he confirmed that Alice had a fine singing voice and Jane spoke French – facts we hadn't know about each other and that he must have heard from his sister or Mother Superior.

Elise and I were sitting farthest from him. As Elizabeth was agreeing that, yes, she was a good horse rider, Elise whispered, "A baby matchmaker. He finds out what we're like so he can fit the baby with the parents."

"They're in it together," I answered.

"I understand you're an artist, Victoria, a painter," Dennis called down the table, flashing a smile. Elise nudged me with her shoe under the table. It was my turn.

"I didn't know that," Emma protested. "What do you paint? Pictures? Will you paint my picture?" She winked at Sarah.

I was saved from answering by Sister Margaret's reappearance at the door. "Dennis, would you please come with me?" Her eyes darted around our table and stopped at me. "Victoria, you, too."

On her bed, Jean lay on her side toward us, eyes closed, her body and gown and sheets a field of white stillness broken by the bright red splotches and gray knife next to her hands.

Victoria's Quest

"I've stopped the bleeding," Sister Margaret said shakily. Her calm public voice was gone.

Now I saw the strips of cloth wound over Jean's wrists. Fresh blood seeped through them like thin red bracelets.

I leaned over Jean, as much as my bulk would allow, and gently eased a tangle of hair away from her face to speak into her ear. "It's Victoria, Jean. Can you hear me? Let me help you."

She stirred, the pulse in her neck quickening. "Where is my baby? I want to die. Let me die," she muttered. Her eyes remained closed.

"Send for Dr. Stephens! Please!" I cried.

Dennis roused himself. "Yes, yes," he said briskly.

Sister Margaret sagged into a chair. The words from Dennis' letter sprang into my mind: *This work has become too heavy a penance for you, dear Margaret.*

After he left, she said, "Victoria, when anyone asks, say Jean had a little extra bleeding after the birth. Nothing to worry about. She needs extra food and rest for a few days."

Yes, I thought angrily, *the only thing you really care about is that Mother Superior and Father Gerald not find out that Jean tried to kill herself.* That was the gravest sin of all and could not happen at St. Mary's Haven.

Now, late at night, after Jean has been soothed with tonics and soup, I am almost exhilarated and eager to write in my log. Having entered into a conspiracy with the Kellys, I have gained a measure of power and a flicker of hope to obtain their cooperation. I have awakened from the stupor I have been in since I arrived. How like it has been to the one I sank into on the island after I finished school, when I felt helpless to control my fate!

Waiting
(Shoreside Light, May 1860 - August 1861)

Papa rowed me and my trunk of meager belongings back to the island on a sweet May morning in 1860 a week after Mr. Briscoe awarded the eighth grade completion certificates. Halfway across, I took a turn at the oars while Papa ate a share of the fried chicken lunch Rose had packed. Pulling the boat on the open water, with gentle waves rippling and mild breezes blowing, I felt a momentary ease of the pain in my heart. The previous summers at the lighthouse had been a round of work and silence, but then there was always moving back to Shoreside to look forward to. Now, there was this summer, with few chances to go to town and no more work at Mr. Briscoe's studio. Then, the long winter marooned, followed by the same for another year, until I was of age and could run away with Paul. How was I going to stand these two years of isolated drudgery with an angry father?

But life with Papa would be different, I discovered that day, after we bumped into the boathouse on the grounds of Shoreside Light in mid-afternoon. As we climbed the hill, I noticed he had not yet started whitewashing the lighthouse, in need of its usual repainting after the harsh winter. Inside, the musty air smelled of burned coffee and wood shavings.

"You can make fresh coffee while I check the tower, Victoria," Papa said.

In the kitchen, my shoes crackled on the sticky floor and a column of greasy black coated the wall above the stove. The dishes and glasses in the cupboard next to the sink were only half-clean. The coffeepot stank, crusted with old grounds. Puzzled at the mess, I tugged up the small window to let in fresh air before opening the door to the pantry to fetch coffee and sugar.

The tiny room no longer looked like a pantry. Curtains made of what appeared to be torn-up sheets hid the open shelves of cans, sacks, and jars that lined the space. A pillow, indented with grimy circles, lay in the center of the floor before a small table that held Papa's open Bible and a carved wooden cross next to a stubby candle.

In a daze, I poked behind the sheet on the left to pull out what I needed. I had scrubbed the pot, boiled the coffee, and set out rewashed cups and spoons when Papa returned downstairs.

"You've seen my chapel, Victoria, I expect."

"In the pantry?" I put on my blank look.

"Yes, that's where I pray, three times a day at least, for your mother's return."

"Oh."

"It took me a long time to carve the cross. Do you like it, Victoria?"

"Yes, Papa." I poured coffee.

Papa stirred two spoonfuls of sugar into his cup and took a long sip. He started talking rapidly then, as if that one swallow had released his voice from months of silence. "Yes, God gave me the message last winter that she will come back and beg my forgiveness. He told me to create a special place of worship to show my faith. I've been a sinner, I know, but she was never satisfied, either. My weakness was buying her that piano. Spent my savings. Near killed me and my men getting it up the hill. I had to limit every penny I gave her because she always wanted pretty foolishness she was careless with. That silver bracelet I bought her. She let you wear it and you almost lost it, remember? She managed to take the bracelet with her, though."

I wanted to remind him I had the bracelet now, it was on my wrist, but he was going on in his strange babble. I wasn't sure whether he was talking to me or himself.

"My father ran away and we nearly starved. She will be glad when she comes back. I wouldn't mind if she goes back to her Catholic faith. It's worshipping God and that's what matters. After she left, I went into town and gave a man money to look for her, I was so desperate. Now, I know she'll come back on her own. I don't need to know where she is. Amen." His torrent of words ended abruptly, like a flash storm on the lake.

I was silent, too, upset and confused by what he said about Mama, and this new Papa who prayed and let the lighthouse go to ruin.

"When is Mr. Mackelhorn's next visit?" I asked, getting up from the table several minutes later.

"Near the beginning of June, I expect." Papa's voice was distant.

"A month will be enough time to get ready," I declared.

Papa shrugged.

The next morning, while Papa was praying, I stomped out to the repair shed behind the boathouse and hauled out cans of whitewash, brushes, rags, and the ladder. At once I started painting the lower part of the lighthouse, now and then making a free hand sketch of a bird or cloud and then brushing over it. Later, Papa came out to watch. "There was no need for that schooling to do the work of the lighthouse, was there, Victoria?" he said with an odd smile.

The following day, he joined me, securing scaffolding to the railing of the lantern room. While I stretched as high as I could from the top rung of the ladder, he painted the upper part, lowering the plank until he could reach where I had ended. The weather was sunny and breezy and the paint dried quickly. I inhaled its rich chalkiness, a pleasant change from the acid fumes in Mr. Briscoe's studio.

By the time the painting was done, Papa had resumed most of his usual duties. Though he still prayed in the pantry for long periods of time, he managed to keep the Fresnel lens going, winding the winches and keeping the tower windows clean. Downstairs I scrubbed walls and floors and polished furniture.

Outdoors again, he patched and scoured the boat inside and out and tidied the boathouse. Meanwhile, I cleaned out the chicken coop and dug out the weeds in the vegetable garden, turned the soil and fertilized it with chicken droppings, and planted tomatoes, lettuce, peppers, and squash. I took down the flag, which was soiled and torn, and washed and mended it. Finally, one day, I washed the bed linen, sheets and blankets, and hung them to dry in the hot sun. The day shone as clear as glass. I looked across the sparkling water at the faint skyline of Shoreside and ached for Paul. If only he could row out to the island! But of course Papa could not know about us.

Mr. Mackelhorn arrived on the tenth of June with a new supply of kerosene, wicks, lumber, and Papa's quarterly paycheck. He was a meticulous inspector of objects, not people. He didn't seem to notice Papa's frequent references to God, only that the lighthouse was bright and tidy, the log in order, and Papa and I wore clean, pressed clothes. Knowing that Mama was gone for good, he hastily ate lunch in the kitchen, while I took care that the pantry door was tightly shut. I was not a much better cook than the first time I had prepared that sorry lunch for him four years earlier. I hoped Paul wouldn't mind my cooking when we were married. After the inspector left, Papa said, "One of these days I'll have to ask Cousin Sherman about hiring a man to be assistant keeper." It was the closest he could come to saying I had saved his position at the lighthouse.

Victoria's Quest

We took turns going into town and, out of the money Papa gave me for groceries, I skimped to buy a supply of paper and pencils. I was able to see Paul on but two of my journeys, when I found him immediately at Willie's and we sneaked away to St. Catherine's. It was hard for me to believe I was seeing him, for all my imagining and thinking of him day and night. He was smiling as always and eager to touch me. As we were leaving, he said, "You seem so far away, Victoria. It seems like you've been out there a year already." His words frightened me, for I feared above all that he would forget me.

When I couldn't see Paul, I spent the little time I had before having to return to the island at the Fogartys. There, nothing seemed to have changed but the worsening of Anna's health. On my last visit before winter set in, she was still sleeping mid-day when I arrived. Maggie's face was long. "She's a bit weak these days," she said as we climbed the stairs and stood together next to Anna's bed. She lay on her side in a patched white nightshirt, breathing rapidly as a cat, with one hand clutching her doll and the other limp across the quilt. Her forehead was beaded with sweat and her rosy skin was chalky white. She didn't waken from the noise of our coming in.

"Have you had the doctor in?"

"Twice." Maggie twisted her apron. "He says she's just the sickly sort."

"There must be something he can do."

Maggie picked up the hem of her apron and gently patted Anna's damp forehead. "Rest, my angel." She turned to me. "It's God's will, Victoria. Come downstairs and have some tea."

During the winter, Papa and I spent most of our time in the parlor, the warmest part of the lighthouse, when we weren't attending to chores. Papa whittled on his current project, a Roman coliseum with an emperor, soldiers, chariots and horses, lions and Christians. He sometimes coughed in the midst of carving and nicked himself, as if in sympathy with the bloodied martyrs emerging from his blocks of wood. Late at night, after I heard Papa snoring, I would sneak one of the wooden creations up to my room to copy. If Papa still thought drawing was a sin, what was whittling but drawing figures with a knife?

While he carved, I knitted indifferently, not seeing the yarn between my fingers, only lost in repetitive motion, thinking of Paul. It took weeks to finish a lopsided afghan for Papa. My work-rough hands constantly snagged on the wool. Before I saw Paul next spring, I would have to soften them with lard.

Mostly, Papa was silent, but there were times he talked and talked as he had that first day I came back to the island. On one such occasion as the wind moaned outside, he said suddenly, "Well, I'm glad you're out of Sherman's household, though Abigail was right about one thing. You and Paul," he said. I shivered, hearing in my head once again his thunderous "you shamed me, you stay away from that boy for good" when Cousin Sherman told him that I had misbehaved.

Papa went on. "Sherman and I grew up near each other out East. His father, Uncle Tobias, was a lawyer and then became a judge. Sometimes he gave my mother money when we had no food in the house. I went to sea and every year gave her nearly all my salary. I could not bear to spend money on myself for anything but necessities. My father, Duncan – your grandfather...." he trailed off.

"What did he do?" I asked quickly. I had never forgotten Papa's rage at my first drawing that somehow had to do with his father.

"What did he do? What did he do?" Papa repeated, jabbing a knife into the flank of a wooden lion. "Oh, he had big dreams, he wasn't content to make his living at the shipyard. No, he had to be an artist. He bought canvases and brushes and painted every day turning out seascapes, he called it. Didn't sell a one, and meanwhile his family was starving. Then one day he runs away. We never heard from him again. *Uff da*, Mother would say over and over, the closest her Norwegian conscience could come to cursing, God bless her. She prayed for deliverance, and God let her go early to her heavenly reward."

Another evening, while snow blistered the lighthouse, he talked about Mama as if he had forgotten who I was. "I was attracted to that woman in a moment of weakness. I should never have allowed that to happen. It was her fault, too, the way she flirted. She knew I was lonely. Every time I came back from delivering a shipment on the Great Lakes, she enticed me until I didn't know up from down. I even thought when I injured my leg, it was meant to be. Then she left, and I am struggling to stay at Shoreside Light. At least, you can't leave me. And she'll be back. I know she will."

After this story, the ghost reappeared, terrifying me with its fluttering rags of white and screeching whine. *What had become of Mama in Chicago? Would she come back? What if she was poorer now than she'd been at the lighthouse? No, that couldn't be. She must be rich and happy now.* I was afraid at any moment the ghost would rip through my bedroom door and pounce on me. Inside, I screamed *Stop! stop!* but it continued its torment until I fell into exhausted sleep.

When Papa went into town for the first time the following April, he came back with shocking news. "Cousin Sherman says a group of men from states that want to secede attacked Fort Sumter in the Charleston harbor in South Carolina."

"What does that mean?" I demanded.

"It means the Stars and Bars of the Confederacy are flying over the fort instead of the Star-Spangled Banner. Cousin Sherman says this is the beginning of real war between the North and South. There is no turning back."

I could hear Cousin Sherman's voice booming, *I tell you, there's no turning back!*

"And war will end slavery," Papa added.

I thought fleetingly of Sadie, now able to live freely; innocent and loving, growing into a young woman like me not far from Shoreside. I had a feeling we would meet again one day. Then, I was thinking only of Paul. Men got killed in war, and he was determined to join the army...

Until it was my turn to go to town and I could see Paul, I sat up late every night, staring out my bedroom window at the dark starry night. *What would I do without my best friend, my love? How would I ever have the life I wanted?* Sometimes, I drew the sky and the stars, the shape of the island, the dark water. Maybe I could persuade Paul not to go.

When we finally met at St. Catherine's two weeks later, I pressed my breasts against his chest and twined my arms around his neck.

"I want to go to war now, but Father wants Michael and me to wait until we're called," he said, leaning down to kiss me.

"We could go instead to Canada," I said, stroking his back with my hands while I moved my lips to his. "That would be a grand adventure, traveling to another country. Wouldn't you like to see what Michigan's like? Think of the whole new territory we'd see on the way to Detroit and over to Windsor."

Paul laughed. "If the war is over by next summer, we might." He tilted his head down at me, his eyes sparkling in the light of the votive candles.

Entry 16 -- 19 Mar. 1868 – Weather: Cold; faint sun

Dear Joseph,
    Yesterday morning there was another birth, unnaturally silent for both child and mother. Jane's son was born dead. Where, oh where, did Dennis take the infant afterwards?! Following her rule of no-complaints, Jane had labored alone all night in her room until Alice knocked on her door for breakfast and heard her groaning.
    "Father Gerald says at least he was able to baptize the baby," Alice told me over the day's wash. She, Jane, and Elizabeth are the only Catholics among us.
    "Does that mean he won't go to hell?" I scoured harder on a sheet's pinkish circles. Jean's, I suddenly realized.
    "Yes," Alice replied seriously, missing my sarcasm. "Ohhh, I ache." She dried her hands on her apron and rubbed the small of her back.
    "We can't work like this much longer, any of us," I said wearily.
    "Jane says at least she can look forward to being a governess and won't have to wash or clean anymore."
    "Hmmmm." I pressed my lips tight to keep from adding, "and in a month she'll be leaving her bedroom door unlocked for Mr. Julian."

    As yet, Sister Margaret allows no one but me to visit Jean. She trusts my discretion. What an irony! This afternoon, I went to Jean's room and found her sitting up in bed, rocking and crooning to her pillow. "My baby is so sweet," she said dreamily, smoothing the wrinkled case as if it were an infant's soft locks.
    "Oh, Jean. That's your pillow, you know that."
    She looked at me without expression, still cradling the pillow. "He's not a hungry baby. No trouble at all."
    I sat on the bed, nearly gagging at her sour breath. "Jean," I tried again. "Your baby isn't here. Someone is feeding him and taking care of him." Gently, I pulled the pillow away and forced myself to put my arms around her. Her

body felt like shifting sand, without will. "You're going to be fine," I said, reassuring myself as well as her. "You just need to get your strength back."

"Sister Margaret says I am a helpless sinner, but if I become a Catholic, I can be forgiven. She holds my hand and prays with me."

"Just keep your thoughts on getting well and strong," I told her, biting my tongue not to rage against this pious judgment of a young woman's suffering.

✳

Dennis comes to the home every Sunday afternoon to visit Sister Margaret, who glows in his presence. She drinks in his face like it's a religious vision. Last Sunday, seeing them through the open parlor door, I had the sudden inspiration to paint his portrait for her. When those rich people in Chicago sat for me, they sometimes unburdened themselves of private worries, as if they were talking to a stranger on a train they would never see again. I desperately needed to find out Sister Margaret's secret, what she was doing penance for. Perhaps it would slip out and I would have the blackmail I wanted. I was not proud of my scheme but it was all I could think to do.

Sister Margaret was delighted with the portrait idea. "Good of you, Victoria! I will give you money for paints and canvas. Please start right away, while you're still able."

"I'll need an easel, and might we use Mother Superior's sitting room? It has the best light." I felt the strangest mixture of excitement and distaste.

Preparing to paint a portrait brought back those two years with Jacob, when I entered into a different bargain with the devil. I was so tired of being poor and so desperate to practice my art. I have to admit a part of me had relished the luxury and ease of my life there.

I may as well go on with that part of my past, the sooner to stop mourning it.

War
(Shoreside Light, Summer 1862)

During another long winter on the island, Papa prayed and whittled and talked about Mama coming back. I stayed as long as I could in the kitchen washing up from meals and doing other chores to delay going into the parlor. I clung to the belief that Paul and I would run away the following summer. I counted on his anticipation of the future and my willing body to keep him faithful. But what if some laughing, lively town girl matched his light heart as well as his steps on the dance floor of the Tavistock?, my middle-of-the-night voice whispered. The only way I could calm my anxiety was to sketch fantasies of a life in Canada –

a snug log house surrounded by wild prairie flowers with snow-capped mountains in the distance.

Only twice did I draw other faces. Once of Anna, after a day of freak warmth melted snow in thin wispy streaks down the kitchen window and reminded me of the white ties of her summer bonnet. Once of Sadie, after a biting wind recalled her shivering the day she arrived at the Fogartys. I'd been so upset about Anna on my last visit that I had forgotten Maggie said there was word on the underground that Sadie had gotten safely to her family and they had moved on to Chicago.

Papa made the first trip into town on an April Saturday. In his absence, I was free to draw outdoors all day long. For an hour at a time, I would forget my worry over the war news he might bring in the joy of drawing a wave, a gull, a rock, the boathouse, the lighthouse itself. I had to force myself to stop for chores and barely finished cleaning the lanterns by the time Papa returned in late afternoon. He'd spent longer than usual at Cousin Sherman's. As he recounted at supper what he'd learned, I forgot my day's pleasure.

"They've fought a terrible battle in Tennessee... A place called Shiloh." Papa hesitated after every sentence as if the words were being forced out of him. "The North was led by General Grant and won... More than ten thousand lives were lost on both sides... In only a few days..." He shook his head.

"Ten thousand!" *The horror of it. Fields and fields of dead bodies, fire and blood everywhere...* I shut my eyes.

"Cousin Sherman says now the Southern armies under General Lee are invading Kentucky, which is neutral, half-Union and half-Confederate," Papa went on, trance-like. "If they get to the base of the Ohio River, they'll bring the war into Ohio and then into Indiana."

"Papa, no!"

"Well, Cousin Sherman is in favor of it." Papa shook his head, waking up a little. "He was in the Mexican War, the Battle of Buena Vista, in 1847 when that rascal President Taylor accused the Indiana men of cowardly retreat. He wants his boys to set the record straight."

I rowed to town the following week and met Paul at St. Catherine's. Our haven that day seemed hateful. The lingering scent of incense I had found pleasing was sickly sweet. The cool air mirrored the icy fear in my soul.

"Don't go, please, my love," I pleaded. Tears spilled down my cheeks. "Let's run away."

"I have to go, Victoria. I have to. Everyone's going. Michael, too. Mother understands, and Father is very proud."

Victoria's Quest

Two months crawled by. I spent as much time as possible outdoors in the summer sun, working in the garden and seeing visions of gray and blue uniformed men shooting rifles and lunging knives at each other in yellow cornfields and thick forests amid booming cannons and agonized screams, Paul smiling as he came face-to-face with a Rebel...

In July, Papa came back with the news that President Lincoln had called for three hundred thousand volunteers for the Union Army. In August, he learned the Indiana governor had ordered the formation of eleven regiments to be mustered in Indiana within three weeks. Shoreside was to be Company G of the 87th regiment. "Cousin Sherman says besides bachelors like his boys and Mr. Briscoe, married men of every occupation in town are joining. He's losing a number of men from Willie's, but he'll make do. Even doctors and lawyers are signing up." *Frank Fogarty won't be going at least,* I thought. *What about Mr. Rankin? If he went to war, would I ever find out where Mama was?*

Paul and I managed to say goodbye two days before Company G's departure on the noon train on August 16. What was there to do but lay together behind the baptismal font of St. Catherine's and again hastily join our bodies?

Oh, Paul's letters. I have kept them all these years. I will take them out of my suitcase and copy them into the log. It won't show his awkward printing and the grimy smudges of his fingerprints on the paper. It also won't reveal his feelings about being cheated of the grand adventure he had dreamed of.

18 August 1862
Monday

Dear Victoria,

Camp Rose — What a name for a place overrun by hundreds of dirty, sweating men! Company G smelled anything but sweet after the long train ride a few days ago. The camp is set up at the county fairgrounds a mile out of South Bend. Men from different companies arrive every day.

Today we had 3 hours of drills. Our company has no trouble keeping up but we don't understand all the orders and rules of the military life. I'm sure we'll learn quickly as soon as we see some action!

Yesterday we had a wonderful treat. Some ladies from South Bend brought a picnic — fried chicken, homemade bread, pickles, pies and cakes, jelly and butter. We gorged ourselves. How could I have taken Rose's cooking for granted? I will send her compliments when I write Father and Mother. We also were preached a Sunday sermon and politicians from South Bend and LaPorte came out in the afternoon to give speeches of congratulations. We haven't done anything yet.

Every night as I go to sleep, I think of you. I am excited about going to war. The rumor here is it will be over, if we do our part, in a few months.

Love, Paul

26 August 1862
Tuesday

Dear Victoria,

Enclosed is a silhouette profile I had cut in South Bend last Saturday when we were allowed to go into town. (This, when I received it, I caressed with my finger — the outline of his head, forehead, nose, lips, chin — and then traced again and again with pencil on my own paper.)

Today we put on a parade for friends and relatives of the men from Winanac and Kewanna. We've been here a week and I thought we did well for drilling only that long. A few men turned left instead of right and I wanted to laugh. Everyone pretended not to notice. The drill sergeant's eyes were bulging out of his head with anger, but he could do nothing in front of the crowd.

Afterwards, we were told to be ready by 5 a.m. tomorrow to depart by train for Indianapolis. The first leg

will be to ride BACK to Shoreside. I have no way to let
you know. I will look out to the lighthouse as we pass.

I got your letter and am glad you are keeping busy on
the island. I wish I could hear you spin one of your
fanciful stories, especially in the dull hours here when I
have nothing to do.

Love, Paul

31 August 1862

Dear Victoria,

It was strange to arrive in Shoreside again so soon
with no one knowing we were on that train. Mr. Roberts,
the train master, was excited and shook every hand he
could reach. We were mighty hungry but had no time to
buy food. We had to hurry to get onto the Monon
Railroad line south to Lafayette. There we did another
change to board the Big 4 line for Indianapolis. We got
finally to Camp Morton, the state fairgrounds north of
Indianapolis. We tore into our dinner of meat, bread and
coffee after nothing all day!

On Saturday we marched into Indianapolis and were
presented officially with an American flag the women of
South Bend had made for us. The ceremony was solemn
and inspirational. I thought of the flag on the island, how
proudly it has waved to the passing ships and boats. I
think all the men felt the same pride and desire to fight
for the Union of our country.

Today our Company G was mustered into service for 3
years. I got $1.50 for enlisting and $13 for the month, the
pay for a private. I am stowing it in a corner of my
rucksack and vow to save as much as I can for you and
me. We were issued clothing — light blue pants, a darker

blue coat, a visored cap with a flat circular top, overcoat, shoes, socks and underwear. Some men have never worn underwear and have to be shown how to put it on!

The rumor is tomorrow we will set off again — to Kentucky. This will be my last letter on Indiana soil. The mail delivery is good so far and I was happy to get your letter of 4 days ago.

Love, Paul

10 September 1862

Dear Victoria,

It seems like months since we left Indiana. When we did so, we had to stay overnight in the railroad cars on account of the rain. Then we had a 9 hour ride with no breakfast to Jeffersonville. We marched through that town to steamboats on the Ohio River. This got us onto Kentucky soil at Louisville. We marched four miles to the county fairgrounds, now Camp Oakland.

For the past 10 days, we have gone on one march after another which made no sense. We find ourselves back to where we started several hours earlier. Someone figured out this must be part of training us to follow orders and make complicated moves. I feel better knowing that. My feet are sore. All of us are hungry. Rations are poor.

The heat is terrible and more steamy than any we've known in Shoreside. I long for the feel of lake breeze. I've been bitten all over by mosquitoes and am feeling a bit under the weather, (joke), on account of this change in activity and locale.

Louisville is strange and most of us don't like it at all. It is a prosperous place and said to be very pro Union. Yet half the people are Negros, most of them slaves. We call

Victoria's Quest

it a 'Secesh' (for Secession) town. It hardens our resolve to fight for the liberty of Negroes.

Due to these silly marches, I am writing you from Jeffersonville. We were ordered back here, who knows why. On our marches we are told to look for the Rebels but we have yet to encounter one. I am excited by that prospect.

Take care of yourself, sweetheart.

Love, Paul

18 September 1862

Dear Victoria,

Here we are back in Louisville. That didn't last long. We continue to go on 10 mile marches to nowhere. Between our knapsacks and the haversacks at our waists we are mightily weighted down.

I am still feeling a bit poorly. I don't mention sickness to anyone. We are close to the action now and I won't chance missing it.

Love, Paul

4 October 1862

Dear Victoria,

We left Louisville 2 days ago at 5 a.m. The weather is very hot and the road dusty as smoke for marching. Some men lightened their knapsacks by dumping items on the road as they walked. However, I'm sure real

Rebels are in the area, not just a pretend group of Confederates.

Kentucky is full of hills and hollows and the road is tight and twisting. We're camped now until early tomorrow morning.

Besides the mosquitoes, there are fleas and chiggers — we spend any free time killing them off. It would help if we could boil our clothes but we don't have the time or water. We're dying of thirst and in great need of sweet water, hard to find in this dry state.

I'm very tired tonight but I'm sure that is part of becoming a hardened soldier. Someone in my tent thinks I should see a doctor but I don't want anyone fussing over me as dear Mother does.

Think of me, Victoria, as I face the enemy at last!

Love, Paul

Those are the six letters he wrote. I answered the letter of October 4 the same as I had the others, sitting outside Strachey's as soon as I received it on my trip to town. I wrote of the little, harmless things of my day – the antics of the gulls, the sunset from the lighthouse tower, the stone castles I made from beach pebbles. I made up a story about him and Sandy and sketched an illustration next to it. I pictured Paul's grin as he read my letter, lying on the ground or sitting near a fire.

I wrote nothing of the turmoil I'd been in when my monthly bleeding did not come. My mind had been afloat with terror. I could not thread one thought to the next over the notion I was with child. Every day felt like I was up to my chin in the lake, struggling to move one foot in front of the other as water sucked around them on the stony bottom. Finally, two weeks later, I saw blood on my thighs in the privy. I wadded the cloth between my legs with relief and thanked the God I did not believe in.

Entry 17 -- 26 Mar. 1868 – Weather: Sunny, light winds

Dear Joseph,

On Tuesday afternoon Sarah, with angry yelps and cursing that horrified Sister Margaret and Mother Superior, quickly gave birth to a baby girl, who took over the chaotic scene with her own lusty-lunged wails. Only a few days ago, while Sister Rosamund's back was turned to the sewing table, Sarah had joked, "We'll get rings on our fingers yet, won't we, Emma?" Mother Superior has arranged her placement as a live-in maid for a rich Catholic family on Michigan Avenue. Sarah says she'll leave as soon as Emma can join her. They're eagerly planning to get rooms and employment together in a downtown store. I don't understand them. But they could not be more excited about their future than I am this afternoon, as the sun pours in and stray green leaves dance by my window!

Yesterday, Elise and I took a walk, a brief one, up and down the street in front of the home, as both of us are easily winded these days. It is an odd but very pleasant feeling to enjoy her company so wholeheartedly. I have been short of women friends. I told her I was going to paint Dennis' portrait.

"That's good, Victoria. Now, you are certainly coming to Philadelphia with me!"

At her words, I stumbled and nearly knocked both of us over. We teetered and swayed, holding each other's arms, until we steadied.

"We're like two elephants," Elise said, laughing a little.

"I'm sorry. I just don't know how I can go with you," I said.

She looked at me with those warm, brown eyes. "I've decided to pay your expenses. I believe – I know – you are going to be famous," she declared.

"I can't do that!" I said, at the same time thinking, *I will, I will!*

We resumed walking, carefully, returning to St. Mary's Haven. "You can pay me back when you sell your first paintings to a big art gallery," Elise concluded. "And in the meantime, you can help me set up my photography studio."

115

As we climbed the steps to the home, she said, "Come to my room and have a few of my chocolates to celebrate," she commanded.

"I can hardly believe this is happening, my friend." I reached over and kissed Elise's cheek. "You are offering me no less than my destiny."

Later... Looking back again to the beginning of this log, I see the despair of my first entries when I felt there was little point to living. I had thought more than once, after giving birth to my child, I would simply walk to Lake Michigan, fill my pockets with stones from the shore, and wade into its cold blue water, out and out and out, until it closed over my head and it was over.

Today – is it only two months later? – I have hope of continuing on the artist's path, learning to be an even better one. This is what I was born to do on this earth, whether or not there is a God who willed it! And adding to – no, doubling – my exhilaration was the letter for me on the mail table this morning. I snatched it up and took it to my room to read. It was the best of all replies to what I had written with my last bit of strength when I arrived here. How I have feared that nothing would come of it! Now, I am told that yes, they will gladly care for my daughter, love and raise her! I will record that much, as cryptically as Papa did events in the lighthouse log. Until I am sure I have managed to get her to them, and I realize it must be with the help of both Sister Margaret and Dennis, I do not want to commit more to paper.

... Still later. I laid down a while, light-headed. I hovered on the edge of sleep, seeing under my lids a vision of wild horses shimmering under a noon day sun on an open plain – a wave of bold, sweating bodies, of thudding hooves, tossing heads, and snorting nostrils. I felt not fear but joy as they rushed by me, the hot breath of the ones closest to me smelling of apples.

Now, sitting at my little desk, I am impatient to finish telling of the War days in Shoreside, of Paul, as terrible as they were. I will reach back, through the years, to connect to what I felt then, the sorrow and the hope, the terror and the excitement that I am feeling now...

Silence
(Shoreside, October 1863)

Nothing from Paul was waiting at the general store when I went to town two weeks after his last letter. Mr. Strachey said cheerfully I would probably get two or three all at once. Two weeks later, close to the end of October, nearly my last trip before winter set in, there was still silence. As I was leaving Strachey's with groceries, Mr. Roberts arrived, frowning, with a telegram in his hand. "This just arrived and I have to get back to the station for the 2 o'clock train. Will you take it to Mr. Sherman Willoughby, Victoria?"

"Yes," I said, fear lashing me like a sudden wave. I gripped the yellow envelope in one hand and held my skirt above my ankles with the other hand and ran blindly toward the factory, several long streets away from the heart of downtown. I felt outside my racing body, with its throbbing heart and ragged breath, as if I were a horse being whipped toward the barn. And there I was, suddenly, in the railroad yard filled with men working and the noise of tools and machinery, still running across the open yard until I reached the brick business office.

I hurtled through the small reception area and into Cousin Sherman's office, startling him at his big desk, piled high with ledgers and papers.

"Well, Victoria!" he bellowed. "What are you doing at Willie's?" He got up and came toward me, his arms open in welcome.

I thrust the envelope toward him like its edge was aflame. "A telegram! Mr. Roberts sent me."

Cousin Sherman grabbed it, ripped it open, and stared at the few lines like a hot-eyed madman. "Oh, my God, my God!! My boy! Dead!" One hand clapped his chest like his heart had burst.

"Who?" I cried. "Who is it?"

"I can't believe it! He died of malaria in a hospital. Michael sent this. He's alive, thank God. But Paul, my dear boy Paul!" He swayed and leaned a hand on his desk, then sank into the visitor's chair next to it, his head in his hands.

I sank to my knees, like I had been hit in the stomach. I could not draw a breath. Cousin Sherman reached a hand blindly toward me to clasp my shoulder. We stayed in that odd tableau, both weeping, for what felt like an hour, though it must have been only a few minutes. Finally, he patted my shoulder a few times and stood up, wiping his face with a large handkerchief from his pocket.

"I must go at once and tell Abigail," he said hoarsely. He helped me to my feet and put his arm around my shoulder. "You must come with me, dear girl, I can't bear this alone. I can't."

The carriage shed stood next to the office. Cousin Sherman shouted to the stable boy to hitch up the horse, and in the next minute I was up in the seat. He slapped the reins hard, and the horse bolted forward out of the side of the yard and into the street. On the swift ride to Front Street, I thought irrelevantly how different this was from the sedate journeys he made to church on Sunday mornings. And with a flash of insight, as Cousin Sherman leaned forward, tears rolling down his red cheeks, crying "it can't be, it can't be, Victoria", I suddenly knew he would have accepted me as Paul's wife – it was only Cousin Abigail who would have shunned me and her son. Now, it didn't matter for any of us.

Michael accompanied Paul's body home on a train from Indianapolis. There were so many people at the church for the funeral that chairs were set up along the back and sides. I remembered nothing of the service, only the minister's monotone reading of verses, the scent of fresh-cut lilies, the slow singing of hymns, and Cousin Abigail's sobbing. Afterwards, in the early November crisp sunshine, Paul was buried with military honors at the new city cemetery on the east side of town. He was the first casualty of the War to be laid to rest there. It was a peaceful place, two acres of grass and trees a distance from the nearest house. I stood with Papa and stared at the open farmland bordering the cemetery, shutting out the sounds of the last words being spoken and everyone else's weeping. Inside, I was screaming, *don't think, don't feel. I have to get away, alone, alone!* As everyone began to walk toward the Willoughbys' house where a meal was offered to the mourners, I told Papa I felt feverish and could not eat a bite and would wait for him at the boat. "Perhaps that's best," Papa agreed, though who he thought it best for I could not tell.

All winter I moved through time and chores as if my body were encased in plaster and my face permanently frozen into blankness. When I spoke to Papa, my voice was little above a whisper. Inside, my thoughts raced like a crackling fire that flicked from one thought to another, random thoughts that I couldn't hold for more than a few moments. I constantly forgot what I was doing – why had I gone to the kitchen or the parlor or the tower room? Like an old woman only alive in the past, I was with Paul at his house, in school, at the stable, on the beach, especially in St. Catherine's... Those memories I lived in, not the present, and the future – what a fairy tale fantasy that had been, I thought wretchedly, like Papa's praying for Mama's return.

Through the winter, cut off from news that reached Shoreside, we knew nothing of the course of the War. Not that it mattered to me. In truth, the only cause I had cared about was that of ending slavery. Whether the states united or split in two didn't seem important enough to lose even one life over. Did Cousin Sherman agree with me now? I was sure Cousin Abigail did. How could they let Michael go back to the War as he was insisting at the funeral? *If they had to lose one son, why couldn't it have been him and not Paul?* I thought bitterly.

In my icy room at night, the wind howling outside, I could neither draw to cheer myself nor sleep to free myself from grief. Though I lay under a thickness of wool blankets, ripples of agitation heated my body like a fever. When my rigid muscles finally let go for an exhausted moment, the ghost swooped in and poked me with cruel, pointed fingers. I tensed to push it away, and agitation flooded me again.

One morning in February, I heard the first crack of ice breaking up on the lake as I got out of bed and shivered into my clothes. Through the window, sun pierced the room, bringing a faint warmth. Suddenly, I remembered my dream from the night before. I recalled few of my dreams, usually waking with the sensation of images just out of mind's reach. In this dream, Paul and I were on a train to Canada. We were laughing and making plans for what we would do when we got there. Then I realized the train wasn't moving. "It'll start up, don't worry," Paul grinned. In the next moment, Paul and the train were gone and I was in my room at the Willoughbys, alone, drawing a faceless picture of Mama.

I crossed the room and knelt in front of the dollhouse. I kept the money I had earned from Mr. Briscoe in an envelope under the rug in the dollhouse parlor. I dumped the contents on the floor. Four one-dollar bills, a quarter, and a nickel. That's all I had. $4.30. Staring at the paper and coins, a fierce anger shot into me. I stood up and looked out the window, first out at the lake and then to Shoreside. "I have to leave. I have to go to Chicago. I have to have money," I chanted, my words growing louder and louder with my rage. The sensation felt so good that I laughed out loud, helplessly, as I used to when Paul tickled my ribs on our way to school that first year. The rage and the laughter magically cleared my mind from its fogged state the same way cloths wiped clean the glass of the tower room.

Victoria's Quest

After a while, I went down to the kitchen to make breakfast. Boiling water for coffee, slicing bread, frying eggs, I thought about the money I needed to get to Chicago. *Fifteen dollars to pay Mr. Rankin for Mama's address. Five dollars for a train ticket? Some money to manage after I arrived and began living the artist's life, whatever that would be.* I wouldn't try to imagine that yet. *Maybe fifty dollars in all?* I smiled to myself. Well, I only needed forty-five dollars and seventy cents then. Of course, I realized, setting the plates of hot food on the table and calling Papa, I could do nothing until the ice broke up and melted enough for us to take turns rowing into town. That was almost two months from now. I began imagining what I would say to Cousin Sherman to ask for a loan. He liked me, and he was generous. I thought chances were good he would be willing. But I would have to tell him what it was for. He might not approve. He might talk to Cousin Abigail about it. He might say he had to talk to Papa about it, and then I'd never get away. I heard Papa's uneven tread coming down the stairs from his room and poured his coffee. Ah, maybe Mr. Briscoe. I was pretty sure he was wealthy, or was it only his parents? But he, too, might feel obligated to talk to Papa about it, not be willing to keep my plans a secret. *How was I going to get the money without Papa finding out? If only I had something valuable of my own to sell. The drawings I stored in the piano had no value. Only famous artists sold their work.*

Then, I gasped. Papa came into the kitchen at that moment. "What's wrong, girl?"

"I spilled coffee on my hand," I said quickly. "It's all right."

We sat down opposite each other at the table and began to eat. I picked at my eggs, secretly exulting over my idea of selling the piano. That should bring enough money for everything I needed. All I had to do was figure out how to arrange it. When Papa was outdoors, I removed my sketches and polished the piano to a high gloss.

In late March, Papa made the first trip to town. A few hours after he left, the supply ship came into view, two weeks early. Here was the luck I needed! Surely, my plan was meant to be. I put on my best dress, re-combed my hair, and pinched my cheeks rosy before scurrying around to make sure everything was in order.

I greeted Mr. Mackelhorn at the door with a wide smile. "My father will be sorely disappointed to have missed you. We were in need of groceries after the long winter. I hope making your inspection with me will be as satisfactory. Perhaps he will return before you must leave. Please come in, Sir."

The inspector stepped into the hallway. "The men will bring in the supply of oil and wicking."

"We're very grateful. Have you spent a pleasant winter in Detroit?"

"Fair enough," he grumped, plucking at his thin gray goatee.

"I have always so admired the important work you do, making sure the lighthouses serve the public safety on the water," I continued in a voice that to me dripped of false flattery but seemed to please Mr. Mackelhorn.

"Thank you," he said, brushing invisible dust from one sleeve. "Not everyone appreciates the service."

I kept smiling and complimenting him as he toured the lighthouse. After examining the log, he put Papa's paycheck on the current page.

After lunch, as he started to get up from the table, I laid a hand on his sleeve and squeezed tears from my eyes. "My mother is very ill, you know."

The inspector jerked his head, his eyes opening wide. "Oh, my. I'm sorry to hear that."

"My father didn't want to burden the lighthouse service with his problems, but I am so worried, Mr. Macklehorn. The debt has run up at the hospital."

Mr. Mackelhorn was silent, smoothing the knees of his trousers.

I kept weeping, calculating my next words. "I thought maybe you would buy our piano as you had always seemed to enjoy hearing Mama play it and you are such a kind gentleman." I smiled through my tears as he cleared his throat and stood up.

"Yes, well."

I crossed the room to him. Steeling myself, I stood on tiptoe and kissed his bony cheek. "That is so wonderful of you."

He turned pink. "Ahem, well, I don't know..."

His men cursed under their breath, hauling the piano down the hill to the ship. "My next visit may well be as early as this time," Mr.

Mackelhorn said slyly when I bid him goodbye. "Your father needn't always be here for the inspection."

I stood waving until the ship was out of sight. When I walked back in the lighthouse, I suddenly panicked. *How was I going to explain to Papa what had happened to the piano?* I paced in the parlor, staring at the empty space, and finally thought of constructing some kind of rough box in the same shape as the piano. It took me some hours hammering together boards, looking out the window every few minutes for Papa's boat on the lake. Finally, I got it done, covered it with the blanket, and swept up the debris. I was up in my room, adding sixty-five dollars to the envelope when Papa stamped into the front hall. My last thought before going to sleep that night was that I had entered my own fairy tale in which I might end up as queen or beggar woman.

Entry 18 -- 30 Mar. 1868 — Weather: Clear and sunny

Dear Joseph,

The sun from the window tinted Mother Superior's drab sitting room a lovely pastel yellow this afternoon when Dennis Kelly settled into a chair and I stood opposite him at the easel. The slightly flowery aroma of his hair pomade overcame the usual scent of lye soap that permeates this and every room in the home from our constant laundering. I asked him to tilt and turn his head in different poses.

"That's the best angle, a wonderful perspective of your face," I exclaimed when he moved into the three-quarters profile I wanted. I had decided beforehand against doing a portrait with those blue eyes, smaller and sharper than Sister Margaret's, fixed on me. His line of vision led straight to Mother Superior's desk against a wall. I could study his face, and he could not study mine.

I stacked several large sheets of paper on the easel and rested my hand, holding a piece of charcoal, across my large stomach. "For this first hour, I'm going to make several sketches before putting paint on canvas," I told him. "Please hold a smile as long as you can, relax when you need to, and then resume the smile. I'll get a fair likeness of your mouth that way."

"The portraits I've seen are serious," he protested, raising his eyebrows in question.

"That's the usual, but I'd like to break the rule for your sister's sake." I made a first stroke, my fingers trembling a bit. "I feel certain she would get great pleasure, which would do her much good, if she looked at your portrait with a happy expression."

"Well, then." Dennis obliged me with an upward crease of his lips – neither a smirk nor a grin – but a composed, contented smile. Some twenty minutes later, breaking the silence, I said I was done and would start to draw the shape of his head. "Not lopsided, I hope," he joked.

123

Victoria's Quest

"Not at all." I smiled, starting on a fresh sheet of paper. "I know it is tedious to sit still, but you may talk as you like now."

He inhaled deeply and sighed. "It's rather nice to be out of the classroom and free of my accounting work as well."

"Accounting?" I asked, putting some rapid strokes on the paper.

"Yes, as a favor, more or less, I do the books for a friend of mine. Mr. Robert Ramsay." His gaze shifted briefly from the desk to the floor.

"I admire your skill in working with figures. I am hopeless at sums." I shook my head, both at my comment and my first messy attempt at an outline. I shifted a fresh sheet of paper on top of it.

"I wouldn't expect it to be otherwise for an artist, but somehow I think you are clever enough at arithmetic." He lapsed into the smooth tone he used talking to St. Mary's Haven women around the table.

"Chicago is a booming city," I said, "You must put in very many long hours." *Good, this try at the shape was better. Some skill was coming back to me anyway.*

"Yes, Mr. Ramsay has done very well," he agreed. "He knew to invest in land and construction."

My attention had been focused on the subject's head and face. Now I took in what he was saying about his employer. Come to think of it, it was strange a religious Brother like Dennis was wearing secular clothing. A maroon suit, expensive and fashionable, it was clear. "It will be interesting to draw your suit when I come to it. It has handsome lines."

Dennis plucked at his sides. "This is a box coat. Robert picked it out for me." As soon as the words were out, his face reddened.

I pretended I didn't notice.

"And where are you from, Victoria?" he asked quickly. "Indiana, isn't it?"

"That's right," I murmured. Mother Superior must have told him. I glanced at her closed desk. *What secrets it must hold.* I remembered that among my false answers in her interview, I had given her a city name different from Shoreside. *But what was it? Started with L, a French name...*

"You and Sister Margaret are natives of Chicago?" I said, stalling.

"Yes, we are a large family, but most have gone elsewhere to make their fortunes and raise their families. Margaret and I are the only ones who remained in Chicago and who did not marry. What city was it in Indiana?" he persisted.

Ah, there, miraculously, the name. "Lafayette," I said.

"Oh, yes, I know of it. It's somewhere near the middle of the state."

"Yes." *My turn.* "Is Sister Margaret well recovered from her illness, would you say? We've been quite concerned about her."

"She takes her duties at the home very seriously," he agreed. "She should rest more."

"She seems to worry a great deal about Jean," I ventured.

The girl is going to be fine," he said sharply. "Margaret is compassionate and pious. She simply wants to give special attention to anyone in need of the church."

"Perhaps that is it," I said. Another period of silence ensued, about fifteen minutes, and then the baby kicked, hard. I couldn't help a moan.

"Are you all right, Victoria?" Dennis got up from his chair.

"I'm fine, but perhaps we'd better stop for the day. It's been nearly an hour."

"Of course, of course. I must get back to my work and you must rest." He folded the easel against the wall while I gathered my paper and charcoal.

"Thank you. We'll meet again tomorrow." *And play our game again,* I thought. *I've won this round, Dennis, and you don't even know it.*

∗

Back in my room, I pulled off my shoes and sank on my bed with relief. I rolled to my side, the only bearable position these days. I closed my eyes, little strokes of charcoal on paper dancing under my lids.

A light tap on the door. "May I come in?" Elise called.

"Please."

"That's the only way I can lie down, too," she said when she saw my prone position. "My ankles are swollen, are yours?"

"Not too badly." I shifted my feet to make room for her. "Come sit here." I motioned to the end of the bed. "I'm back from my first session at the easel with Dennis Kelly."

"Oh, how did it go?"

"I feel like the mouse trying to keep away from the curious cat."

Elise laughed. In advanced pregnancy, she was more beautiful than ever. Her porcelain skin had a shell-pink glow, and her rich brown hair, with soft tendrils escaping at the temples, gleamed in the light. Her skin smelled faintly of rose water. "I told you he was a baby matchmaker. He wants to know everything about us."

"Well, there is some information I would like to keep in my possession," I complained.

Elise patted my ankle. "I don't mean to make light of it. I don't want to tell Dennis Kelly my life story, either. I went to great lengths to keep my presence here a secret from everyone."

"I did the same, though there are few to wonder where I am."

"My mother is dead, as you know," Elise went on, twisting a few strands of hair around her finger. "My father is gone as well." She paused. "And something else terrible, as terrible as death, happened to me after that. May I tell you, Victoria, now that you and I are going to go on to the next phase of our lives together?"

Victoria's Quest

"Of course." I nodded, dread prickling my skin like needles.

Elise bowed her head and her voice lowered to nearly a whisper. "After Mother's death, I was consumed with settling my financial affairs. The family's longtime advisor, Mr. Barnes, went over everything with me. He was a bachelor, nearly as old as my father but wiry, with a perpetual sneer on his face. Many times I had noticed him watching me with what I thought was disapproval."

"It was admiration, I'm sure."

Elise looked at me, her eyes full of pain. In a slow, hesitant voice, she said, "One day... no one else was in the house... he came over to me... pulled me to a sofa and ... forced me to yield to him. A pain so terrible, so bloody..."

"Oh, Elise, my dear friend." Horrified, I sat up and put my arm around her slender shoulders, my head swaying back and forth in disbelief at this hideous revelation.

Elise leaned her head against mine. "Somehow I got myself upstairs and to bed. He never came back, and I eventually learned he had left town the very next day. By then I knew I was pregnant."

"How on earth have you kept your sanity?" I asked, knowing how close I had come to losing mine.

"By believing the future will be better. Even happy," she said simply.

"After this is all over?"

"I am already living in the future, in Philadelphia," Elise said, her voice resuming some of its usual confidence.

"Yes, I'm there with you, too," I agreed, stilling my doubt this was a fantasy like the one I had about my wonderful life with rich Mama in Chicago.

Leaving Shoreside
(April 1863)

Time that had inched like a snail through the past months soared like a bird on wing the week after Mr. Mackelhorn bought the piano. I had determined I would leave the island for good the following Saturday when it was my turn to go into town. I was two selves, one doing chores and talking to Papa in the daytime, the other scheming by candlelight late at night in my room. There was little of a practical nature I needed to do, other than fashion a cloth sack from burlap to hold my belongings – clothes, a few photographs, and Paul's letters. Between my dresses, I nestled the drawings, rolled up and tied with string, that I

126

judged best of what I had done. I took one other thing – one of Papa's carved horses. That was everything, except for the envelope of money.

One afternoon in mid-week, I found myself singing, just as Mama had before she disappeared. That evening after supper, I listened to Papa, muttering through the pantry door as I washed the dishes, and didn't know if I could stand to wait until Saturday to leave.

On Friday night, the ghost appeared in a playful mood, sliding under my door and dancing around my bed, gleefully fluttering its bodiless white sleeves across my face. Finally, I got out of bed, lit a candle, wrapped a shawl around my nightgown and went outdoors. The wind blew out the candle but there was enough moonlight to wander around a bit, to see my way to the vegetable garden – *would Papa keep it alive?* – and then down to the shelf of rocks where I had so often kept company with the gulls. The smell of the lake air at night was sweet. I scraped my bare feet on some loose stones. At last I went back to my bed where I stayed awake, thwarting the ghost's return by holding a single image in my mind, painting at the easel.

Just before dawn, I dressed and once again crept out of the lighthouse, this time hurrying down the hill with my sack to the boathouse. As light thinned from black to gray, I eased the rowboat onto the open water and set off, dipping the oars quietly until I was well away. Once or twice, I stopped and looked over my shoulder at the dark island with the glow in the tower. Soon, Papa would wake, light the first lantern, and discover the note on the kitchen table saying I had left early on the trip to town. I rowed hard against a sudden wind that blew up and churned the waves. My body swayed back and forth in time with the slapping oars, and I fixed my eyes straight ahead on the town as it grew larger and larger. The sun came up, too weak to warm the early morning air, flickering among low clouds like a giant candle.

Arriving at Papa's aging and wobbly little dock, I was glad to tie up the boat and step onto the beach out of the wind. On the other side of the scrub pines, several yards away, I heard people's voices and the clatter of wagons and carriages on Front Street. The bells in St. Catherine's tower chimed eight as soon as I set off up the beach toward the town cemetery. I recognized Eighth Street by some of the houses and crossed through the pines onto the end of the street and made my way to the black wrought iron entrance to the cemetery.

Victoria's Quest

Inside the gate, the bare-limbed oak and sycamores of last November boasted the new green leaves of spring. A thin layer of grass sprouted over the hardened earth of Paul's grave beneath a large limestone marker. Cousin Sherman and Cousin Abigail must have chosen it with such sorrow. I stooped close to the stone and traced with a finger the name and years of birth and death and the words "Gone to Rest" under the hands. Rest – that had rarely been Paul's wish, he had wanted adventure. I found a stick, dug a small hole, and buried the tiny wooden horse. It would be Paul's companion in whatever world he had gone to. I let out a sob, imagining him smiling at this idea. Then I got to my feet. I must not linger or I'd lose my nerve and Paul wouldn't want that. *I'll come back again,* I silently promised him. On my way out, I saw what I'd been too hurried to notice before, six new graves of Civil War soldiers.

When St. Catherine's struck nine, I was waiting at the door of Campbell's Detective Agency. The sign was in the window and everything looked the same as it had three years earlier. But the office was dark and empty. *Where was Mr. Rankin?* I paced up and down the street and around the block several times, avoiding the stares of men in the other shops. *Should I look for him at the train station? Was he even in town? What if he was away the whole weekend? I couldn't stay in Shoreside and be found out.*

Finally, at ten-thirty, as I was close to giving up, Mr. Rankin arrived at the end of the street. If he was surprised to see a young woman waiting for him, he showed no sign of it.

"Good morning," he said a minute later, unlocking the office door.

"Good morning. I have the money," I said in one breath, following him inside. He smiled, sat down at his desk, and smoothed his red mustache. "What's the name again?"

"Kathleen Flinn Willoughby." I handed him the fifteen dollars. Without delay he reached into a cabinet drawer and took out Mama's file.

In a careful script, he wrote first a receipt for me and then Mama's address. "Well, now, this address might not be right," he said. "I got it some time ago. I'll check with Chicago headquarters on Monday."

I clutched the paper. "I'll go ahead and take this and come back next week sometime to make sure," I said quickly.

He scanned my blank face. "If she has moved, it's probably not too far away," he said. "This is an Irish area to the south of downtown. They call it Conley's Patch."

As soon as I was out of sight from his window, I ran to the depot in time to buy a ticket for the 11:30 a.m. train to Chicago.

Entry 19 -- 8 Apr. 1868 – Weather: Strong winds abating

Dear Joseph,

Around St. Mary's Haven yesterday the wind raged, slamming doors and hooting down chimneys, keeping up its tirade into the night. In my room, I lay awake, my thoughts twisting and turning with the baby shifting in my belly, panicked about securing the help of the Kellys. A few hours earlier, I had finished Dennis' portrait, exulting in its completion but despairing of ever learning Sister Margaret's secret. For after the first session of painting, I found I could not work and at the same time talk with Dennis in a calculating way. Gripping the brush between my fingers, splaying its bristles in pressing the dabs of paint on the palette, staring at my subject across the room, I did not know anything but the effort of my hand and eye to transfer my vision onto the canvas before me. I did not know the passing of time, only the smell of paint and turpentine and the sensation of light and motion. My consciousness was only in creating a likeness of the man's features, the planes and shadows of his face, his expressive mouth, his keen eyes, that would make his sister exclaim when she saw it, "Yes, Victoria, this is my dearest brother!"

I stared at the ceiling, covering my ears with my hands against the wind's belligerent rattle at the window, an echo of trying to shut out the lighthouse ghost, my mind repeating, *I'm out of time, I'm out of time.* Finally, I forced myself to breathe slowly, in and out, to soothe my panic. *Calm down. I should have another week at least before giving birth. Think, think.* Sister Margaret was not well liked by the other sisters. If I was clever, maybe one of them would let the truth slip out. If only I had been more pleasant in my dealings with the nuns over the past months. I had never said more than a few words to any of the teaching sisters, least of all Sister Margaret's shy roommate, Sister Winifred. They kept to themselves, anyway, taking meals at their own tables in the dining hall, gone the rest of the day at school, off on weekends to duties at St. Mary's Cathedral.

Victoria's Quest

That left Sister Rosamund, Sister Barbara, and Reverend Mother. I did not think I could ask shrewd Mother Superior questions, no matter how subtle, without arousing her suspicion and making trouble for myself. I doubted Sister Rosamund knew anything useful. She had come to St. Mary's Haven only last year, replacing a nun who had fallen ill with tuberculosis. That left timid, plump Sister Barbara. *Hmmm.* I recalled she and Sister Margaret had been novices together, though they were not friends at the home. *And didn't Alice, who likes to sit in the kitchen, say Sister Barbara was a gossip?*

I sighed, with a little moan, not knowing if it had taken me a few minutes or an hour to arrive at the obvious. But at last I could close my eyes and take my hands from my head and let the wind howl as it would, as I sank into welcome unconsciousness.

The last few weeks before our babies are due, we are excused from the heavy laundry work. Instead of joining the others at the wash tubs after breakfast this morning, I returned to my room. Elise had given me a half-dozen of her chocolates. I had eaten only one since. Its rich sweetness had turned my stomach. Mid-morning, I took the rest of the candy to the kitchen. Sister Barbara was muttering as she fed cut-up vegetables to a stew pot on the stove.

"Sister, may I interrupt you a moment? I've brought you something. A little thank-you for your cooking." I closed my nostrils to the pungent steam of turnips and onions.

"Oh, my." The nun kneaded her wet hands on her apron and eagerly crossed the room to see my gift. "Chocolates! How lovely! Well, now, this calls for a cup of tea to go with. I didn't have much breakfast this morning. Will you join me?"

"Yes, thank you." I sank heavily into a chair at the kitchen table. I felt hot, though the heat of the stove did not reach this far and the air was cool.

As she went about making tea, I told her how grateful the girls were to be in St. Mary's Haven. "The three of you – I mean Sister Rosamund, Sister Margaret, and you – work so hard," I said, intending to move toward questions about Sister Margaret.

Sister Barbara carried over two cups of tea and sat down. Her resentful reply was not what I expected. "Reverend Mother is hard to please, that's why we're running day and night. Did you know her name is Sister Vincent Marie? She's French. Fussy." She opened the sack, plucked one out, and bit into it. "Umm. Delicious. Caramel."

"That's interesting. I did notice some sort of accent." I swallowed some tea to cover my smile at Mother Superior's refined palate coping with Sister Barbara's cooking.

"Yes, people don't realize the order came from France. Little Sisters of St. Paul. They brought it to America, St. Louis. Here, we're mostly German or Irish, though," she said.

"Which are you, Sister?" I fanned my perspiring face with one hand.

"German." She finished the chocolate with satisfaction. "You've had my strudel, haven't you?"

"Yes, indeed." *The not quite cooked apples and vinegary syrup, the dry floury pastry you have to saw with a knife...*

"Did you learn to cook from your mother or after you became a nun?"

"After. I heard the call very young, barely sixteen. That's the age Reverend Mother prefers."

"Is that when Sister Margaret came in, too?"

"No, she was over eighteen." Sister Barbara gazed lovingly into the candy box. "Wouldn't you like one of your chocolates?"

"No, please enjoy them. I'm not at all hungry... I wonder why Reverend Mother thinks age matters."

"Little chance of sinning with a man that way, she says." Sister Barbara raised another chocolate to her mouth.

"Doesn't the church offer forgiveness to all sinners?" I asked. *I was not yet sixteen with Paul in St. Catherine's. Had Sister Margaret been in love at the same age?*

The nun shook her head. "Reverend Mother doesn't think that applies to nuns. She's told us over and over that if she knew any of us had done what you girls have, she'd force her to leave the order."

"Of course, she doesn't suspect such a thing, does she?" I murmured. Beneath my dress, the cotton shift had turned damp from the sudden heat of my body.

"Oh, *she* doesn't."

In the heavy silence that followed, we drank our tea and Sister Barbara ate her chocolate.

Finally, I put a hand on her sleeve and smiled. "To know one of you good sisters has been forgiven for the same sin would give me such hope and comfort," I said as sweetly as I could.

Sister Barbara hesitated, then with a faint smile looked beyond me to the kitchen window. "Then, think about who is there when each baby is born, who is first to make sure the baby is given away, and I don't mean the Reverend Mother," she said, licking the chocolate from her fingers.

I've been writing this half lying in bed, guilt over what I'm doing having brought on nausea and fatigue so great I can't sit at my desk. And still I will

Victoria's Quest

keep writing. Memories of the past push at me relentlessly, demanding to be told now before I come to the end of this part of my life's journey. Hope is being reborn again in Chicago – hope dashed, hope reborn, hope dashed, such seems to be my story...

Mama
(March 1863)

A t last, I was on the train to Chicago! I had dreamed of starting a new life in that city and now I would arrive by nightfall.

"Quite a journey for a young lady," Mr. Roberts had said twenty minutes earlier when I bought my ticket. "There can be rough men on the train. Be sure you sit in the ladies' car, the last passenger car. No smoking in there either. There's plenty of dust and cinders without cigar ashes and fumes." Luckily, the Michigan Central pulled in as he seemed about to ask why I was going, and then he was too busy supervising the unloading of freight cars to say anything more.

When I climbed the stairs into the back of the ladies' car, some heads had turned, nodded at my brief smile, and turned back to their conversations. I sat next to the window and settled my sack on the empty seat next to me. With all the seats facing forward and the wood-burning stove in the middle, the car reminded me of Mr. Briscoe's schoolroom, the difference being the low white ornamented ceiling, door at each end, and row of windows on each side. Gas lamps on the panels between the windows only dimly lit the car, and the heat from the stove barely warmed the air. The sunny spring day outside had disappeared. I shivered from cold and excitement.

Ahead of me sat a dozen or so other women, chatting in pairs on the double seats. I heard an exchange between two well-dressed ladies about staying in the same downtown hotel. Some of the plainly dressed women were traveling with children, perhaps wives joining husbands who had gotten factory jobs or were gathering supplies to strike out West from Chicago. A few other women sat alone like me, including one in a black gabardine dress and black straw bonnet who looked restlessly around as if she wanted something to do. Across the aisle from her, a sleeping woman in a light green dress and feathered hat woke up as the train left the depot. The tracks went north a few blocks through town until close to the shore line and then turned west to parallel Lake Michigan. I caught a last glimpse of the lighthouse, which looked no different after my abandonment of it this morning. Papa did not yet know I was gone for good.

As the train picked up speed, the woman in the feathered hat leaned toward the woman in the black bonnet. "Isn't it adventurous to ride the train? I'm from Detroit. I will visit relatives in Chicago. Might you be visiting family, too?"

The women turned her head toward her questioner and I saw her strong profile under the bonnet. "I am going to do some nursing work," she said in a clear voice.

"Oh, you're a nurse. How interesting. Which hospital?"

"I'll be on the south side at Camp Douglas, a training ground for Union soldiers. Now they are holding Confederate prisoners there, too."

The woman in the feathered hat drew back a little. "You are very adventurous."

"I am needed there," the nurse said simply.

They fell silent and, my buoyant mood momentarily lost, I shifted my attention to the lake outside the window and the steady traffic of vessels in both directions. I hadn't thought about war in this part of the country, Illinois and Indiana. The battles I'd heard about took place in the South or in the East. Yet there was a prisoner of war camp in the middle of Chicago! And, of course, men on both sides were continuing to fight, to be wounded and to suffer, to die. The War had not ended because Paul was in his grave.

A bit of sun sparked the silver of my bracelet. I smoothed the links, wishing I could move the hours forward to my reunion with Mama. I called up my old dream of her return to Shoreside, sweeping me out of the Willoughbys after announcing to the far less fashionably dressed Cousin Abigail that she was taking me to Chicago to join her in the life of a true lady, such as was unavailable to any in a small Indiana town. And soon after, of our strolling the most elegant avenues of the city, looking in fine store windows, stopping for an afternoon pastry and tea in a smart hotel.

Now, I imagined her awaiting me in an immense and beautiful mansion filled with admirers, laughter, and music. When the maid opened the door, and she arrived a moment later, curious about the young female stranger calling on her, I saw her embrace me, tears of joy and wonder in her eyes at my miraculous appearance. I saw myself hugging her in return, but holding back a while to show I hadn't forgotten her betrayal, that she had some mending to do that would require some humility and time, and then holding out my wrist in forgiveness to show her the bracelet, the unbroken connection between us, whereupon we would both weep. Later,

Victoria's Quest

I'd show her my drawings, and she'd swoon in amazement at my talent and say she was so happy I hadn't let Papa's disapproval stop me from developing my skill. I'd tell her I had in fact come to Chicago not only to see her but to become an artist, and she would say she had many friends in the art world she would introduce me to, and there was the perfect room for my studio in her house. In light of our new relationship, after all I was sixteen, I would stop calling her by the child's name of Mama. Silently I tried it out. *Mother. Hello, Mother. How are you, Mother? You look well, Mother.*

I sighed and closed my eyes, suddenly exhausted from nerves. I dozed a while in an uncomfortable half-sleep until the conductor slammed the door entering our car from the one in front. He had a gray mustache that matched his gray uniform and cap. Collecting tickets, he made an unsteady but dignified way down the aisle against the lurching of the train. When he took my ticket, I held out the piece of paper Mr. Rankin had given me.

"Can you tell me where 65 Wells is, please?"

He cocked his head and squinted at the paper. "Wells is a main street somewhere downtown, Miss, that's all I know. Get off at the last stop and ask someone." He moved on briskly.

After a while, I ate a few bites of the bread and cheese I'd packed in my sack. I was looking forward to a hot supper at Mama's – Mother's – house. As a change from the lake view, I looked out the windows on the other side of the train. Over the next hour, the vista of cropland and scattered farmhouses slowly gave way to that of widely separated villages, and then to the edge of what seemed yet another village. It did not end but continued, muddy street after muddy street of shacks and tiny houses and then row houses, stores, and people everywhere, walking on planked sidewalks or riding on horseback or behind teams of horses pulling carriages or oxen pulling wagons, many times busier than the streets of Shoreside. "We're coming into the city," a woman said loudly, and the well-dressed travelers began checking through their packages and bags to make sure they had everything and pointing to the sights out the window. *Closer and closer to my mother*, said my heart in rhythm with the wheels of the train.

The conductor called out a street name as the train stopped at an open shed. The women with children hurried off and were met by some men with wagons piled high with furniture.

Not long after, the train halted again, this time in front of a vast field of tents. "Cottage Avenue – Camp Douglas," the conductor announced. Calmly, the nurse left the car, and we watched her carrying a black suitcase to a gate guarded by an armed sentry. Beyond him, other soldiers were herding a line of ragged, skinny men along a swampy path toward a large, nearly windowless wooden building. The woman in the feathered hat crossed herself.

As the train moved north, apartment and office buildings appeared, and the streets were even more crowded with people, animals, and vehicles. Then, the train slowed, and I saw the wide tranquil avenue of mansions from my dreams. That could be Wells!

The next thing I knew, the conductor was bustling through the car crying, "Downtown Chicago. End of the line. Everyone off!" Like an exhausted beast, the train shuddered to a final hissing stop, and I was standing, legs trembling and stomach knotted, at the back of the car, the first to step down into the street.

Men were already unloading goods from the freight cars into an enormous open shed which seemed to offer no conveniences to travelers. The shout of voices and rumble of barrels and crates added to the din of snorting horses and clattering carriage wheels. The street stank of manure and garbage, the odor blown fully into my face by the wind. Turning to see the lake was but a short distance east, I paused at the sight of an enormous freighter and, when I turned back, the other passengers had disappeared in the crowd. Mud was splattering from wheels and hooves onto my dress, and I hastily stepped up on the planked sidewalk full of more people. Feeling invisible to their unfriendly faces, I decided to walk back in the direction of the mansions I'd seen from the train. As I hurried along, I heard scrabbling sounds under my feet and nearly screamed when some plump, brown rats jumped out and scurried for garbage in the streets. Clutching my sack and almost running now, I soon came to the first block of large homes and gardens and nearly ran into an elderly man in a bowler hat coming from the opposite direction. "Good afternoon, Miss," he said with a kind smile, tipping his hat.

"Good afternoon, Sir. Might this be Wells?" I asked with as much confidence as I could muster.

"Oh my, no, young lady. This is the one and only magnificent Michigan Avenue!" He beamed until he saw my frown.

"Yes, well, let me think a moment. Wells, Wells..." he gazed upward, tapping his generous lip with a gloved finger, and said, "I have it now. Turn right at this corner, which is Randolph, and keep walking three or four blocks to Courthouse Square. There's a fountain in the middle. Wells should be one more block beyond that."

Victoria's Quest

I thanked him and hurried off. Wells didn't sound so far, like walking from one end of Shoreside to the other. I just hoped he was right about the route.

He called something after me in a warning tone – "neighborhood" was the only word I heard. I was already too far away. I wanted to reach my mother's house before dark.

When I arrived at the square, only men seemed to be coming and going, big and prosperous looking men like Cousin Sherman. I kept my head down, not wanting to be noticed until I got to Wells. It must be an important street if it bordered the city government buildings. But the next block of Randolph did not look any different from the street where I had gotten off the train, and as I turned down Wells looking for number 65, I passed only boardinghouses, a livery stable, shops, and several taverns, some of which had their windows covered with dark curtains so no one could see in. People's loud talk and laughter amid live music seem to come from every door and window. My mind began to race. *How could my mother be living on this street? Had I gone in the wrong direction and her address was not south, but north on Wells?* I stumbled on, staying on the outer edge of the sidewalk, searching for numbers. Some buildings had one, some didn't. 21, 33, 37, 39, 45, 61... I stopped dead at number 65. O'Keefe's Tavern was the painted green sign over the door.

My mother must own it and live somewhere else, I thought wildly. *Mr. Rankin had only found her business address.* Holding desperately to this thought, I plunged through the door and into a place heavy with the smell of beer, cigar smoke, and fried pork. Men stood at a wide bar along the wall and hunched around small round tables, talking and arguing. Someone was pounding boisterous tunes on a piano at the far end of the bar. No one looked up except the light-haired bartender, who gave me a friendly nod. He would know where my mother was. I would buy a glass of cider from him. When I got closer to him, I glanced at the piano player, a woman in a low-cut gold dress and glittering jewelry, just ending a tune with a thumping flourish of the keys. At that moment, a heavy man with a mug of beer put on a hand on her bare shoulder. "C'mon, Kate, baby, play some more songs."

The woman shrugged off his hand and stood up. "In a little while, Joe." Her voice was hoarse. "I'm taking a break."

She turned and her glazed eyes focused uncomprehendingly on me. It was Mama.

I staggered back and stared at her.

"Well, what are you looking at, I don't have two heads, do I?" she slurred.

"Don't you recognize me, Mama?"

"Mama?" she repeated as if she had never heard the name.

"Yes, it's Victoria. Your daughter!" I cried.

She put a steadying hand on top of the piano and stared at me. "I don't think so, girlie. My Victoria is a little girl."

"Six years ago when you left, I was a little girl. Now, I'm sixteen," I said, holding my sack tightly to my chest.

"Six years?" she echoed with confusion. "Have I been in Chicago that long?"

"What has happened to you, Mama?" I cried again.

She swayed as if I'd knocked against her. "How did you get to Chicago and find me?" she asked in a quieter tone.

"I sold the piano and a detective got your address," I said loudly.

"Do you have the law with you?" She looked anxiously toward the door, and the man with the mug of beer laughed.

"No!" I stamped my foot. "Aren't you glad to see me?" I demanded.

At my outburst, she hastily said, "Of course, of course. A wonderful surprise." She put her arms around me and called over my shoulder to the bartender. "Hey, Dennis, see who's here."

I pulled out of her embrace as the man leaned over the bar, grinning and looking me up and down. His eyes were green.

"Remember my little Victoria?"

"Well, well, how she's grown." Before I knew what was happening, he kissed me wetly on the lips.

"Now, none of that, Dennis Flanagan," my mother said, punching his shoulder with a short laugh.

Dennis Flanagan! Mama's childhood friend who lost his boat and stayed at the lighthouse and talked about Chicago. It was all so simple and so horrible. They had run away here and this is what had become of them, working in a rough tavern.

Dennis heaved two mugs of beer on the counter in front of us. "How about a drink on the house then for your long lost daughter?" He winked at Mama.

"Yes, Victoria, let's celebrate," Mama said gaily, taking a swig of beer.

But I was already halfway across the room.

"I hate you, hate you, hate you," I screamed, and ran into the street.

Entry 20 -- 9 Apr. 1868 — Weather: Still windy

Dear Joseph,

I am nearly in the same feverish state of excitement as I fell into yesterday. It drives me to record the rest of what happened, the meeting with Sister Margaret that may ensure my baby's future. And I must finish the log, end this chapter of my life before I give birth. In Philadelphia, I will start a new one that will read far differently than this!

After I left Sister Barbara in the kitchen, I went looking for Sister Margaret and found her in the hall just leaving Jean's room.

"Shhh," she said, a finger to her lips. "I've just settled her down." She took off her glasses and rubbed the deep marks on the bridge of her nose. Her puffy lids hung over unnaturally bright eyes. Her rumpled habit looked slept in.

"Is she better? It's been some days since I've come to see..."

"*Much* better," she interrupted. "Jean is becoming a Catholic, and Reverend Mother has arranged for her to live with a family in the church who'll be kind to her and not expect too much."

"She has accepted her child's... absence?" I inhaled sharply. The baby had pushed against my ribs as if she heard.

"Yes, and that she must not look for him, ever." The nun's emphatic voice assumed its old irritability.

"Jean's regained her health," I said, "but are you well, Sister Margaret? You look in need of rest."

"Nonsense," she said gaily. "I am full of energy. Prayer and penance, that's how God saves us, as I've told Jean many times." She crossed her arms and inserted them in her sleeves, rocking on her heels.

I gave her a bright smile. "I finished your brother's portrait. Would you like to see it?"

"Yes, of course!"

Victoria's Quest

When we came into my room, I closed the door behind us. Together, we stood in front of the portrait, propped on the easel at the foot of my bed. "Dennis was pleased. I hope you are, too," I said.

"That's his smile!" Sister Margaret exclaimed. "In the next moment, he's going to say something humorous and make me laugh." She giggled like he had made a joke right then.

"His features were a pleasure to paint." Yet, looking at the portrait afresh, I was taken aback to see that somehow I had painted a cunning glint in his eyes and a domineering twist in the smiling lips.

"The maroon suit looks well on him." Sister Margaret was admiring other details.

"Very fashionable these days, I believe."

"Reverend Mother allows us to have family pictures in our rooms. This may be a little larger than most. I hope Sister Winifred won't mind." She beamed, then turned from the portrait to look at me. "I remember the day I came upon you sketching, a piece of jewelry of some sort. I could see your talent. But this! You truly have a gift, Victoria." Her habit rustled as she gestured back at the portrait with wide arms.

"Thank you." Despite my nervousness, I was pleased by her compliment.

Her voice turned serious. "My brother and I simply can't accept this without some compensation for you. It is too fine. You may keep the easel and paint and materials, of course, but I shall talk to Dennis about a payment. He can afford it."

Or Robert can. Fortunately, I only thought this but did not say it aloud.

Sudden nausea forced me to sit on the bed. With the opportunity before me to set my plan in motion, I didn't know whether I could do it, if I could be so cruel.

I spoke quickly before I could change my mind. "That is very kind, Sister. A payment would be welcome, but not one of money."

"Oh?" She frowned at me suspiciously.

"Please, would you sit a moment and hear me out?" I pulled at the wrinkles of the blanket to make a smooth place for her. And, in that moment, when she sat down with an apprehensive look, and I knew the effect of what I would say, I felt power shift like an invisible magnet from her to me.

I spoke calmly though my stomach churned. "It has to do with the home my baby is placed in, Sister. There is a family in Chicago I would like her to be taken to. A family I know who will love her and are willing to raise her."

The nun stiffened. "That's against the rules," she said abruptly. "I'm sure Reverend Mother told you that when you came in."

"The other women don't know anyone personally who wants to take their child. I do," I insisted.

Sister Margaret's voice became rote as if she were saying a Hail Mary. "Reverend Mother believes it's best for the church to decide the best home for each baby born under these unfortunate circumstances."

"The church," I repeated, "meaning your brother?"

"Dennis?" The nun's good left hand fumbled for the rosary hanging from the belt at her waist.

"Sister, please, it's no secret to the women here that Dennis Kelly has an important voice in deciding on the adoptions. The questions he asks when he visits, and he's been seen taking away babies in the middle of the night."

"Who? Who's seen him?" She looked toward my door as if she expected the accuser to be on the other side.

When I didn't answer, she said loudly, "Anyway, that is none of your concern."

"None of our concern – who will parent our babies?" I echoed, patting my belly for emphasis. "Your brother's recommendations may well not be the best, considering he is not and never will be a parent himself."

"Whatever do you mean, Victoria," Sister Margaret said sharply. "You don't know that."

"I understand how close he and Mr. Ramsay are." I looked her in the eye, and she turned her head away toward the portrait as if protecting her brother from what I was saying. When she turned back, she murmured, "Really, Victoria, you aren't making any sense at all."

"Sister, all I'm asking for is an exception, that my baby goes to the home I want." I tried to smile.

She hoisted herself to her feet. "I'm very disappointed in you, Victoria. This is hardly a fair compensation for a painting."

I stood up to face her and took a breath. *Now or never.* "Sister, I thought *you* of all the sisters would help me. *You* – who also had a baby outside of marriage."

The nun swayed, and I reached out to steady her arm. She pulled away and snapped, "I can not believe the terrible accusations you are making."

Pretending she had confessed, I said firmly, "Your secret remains safe for now, but I may not be able to keep it forever. And it's Reverend Mother, of course, who must never know."

Sister Margaret looked at me with horror, tried and failed to speak. Tears slid down her cheeks.

"I'm sorry, Sister, but you see I am desperate, too. If you help me, no one will ever know, I swear to God." I couldn't let myself care about her misery. Her child's fate was decided. Mine was not.

Choking back sobs, Sister Margaret took her brother's painting from the easel and left without another word.

143

Victoria's Quest

After a few minutes, I crept over to the basin, poured water from the pitcher into my cupped hands, and splashed it over my face. I had done it, what I had to. Desperate was the word I used with Sister Margaret. Desperate as I was the day in Chicago I had no other choice but the one I made.

Jacob Hoffman
(Chicago, March - September 1863)

I met Jacob Hoffman on an early June afternoon two months after my arrival in Chicago. I had wandered far out of my neighborhood and was sitting on a bench at the lakeshore, sketching the incoming waves, imagining them flowing southeast to Shoreside Light. I was so lost in my vision I was at first annoyed rather than alarmed when a shadow fell over my page. I looked up to see a well-dressed, middle-aged man with a brown beard peering sideways at my drawing pad.

"You are an artist," he stated. His eyes were small but intense, with lashes like awnings shielding their brightness. His nose was broad, his lips full, sensuous as a rosebud.

"Thank you." Looking down again, I hunched over my paper and added a few lines, hoping he would go away.

"May I introduce myself? Mr. Jacob Hoffman," he continued.

I nodded, glancing to see if other people were nearby in case I needed to call for help.

"Your seascape is charming."

"Thank you." I stood up and opened my satchel to put pencils and pad away. "I've done others of Lake Michigan but only in Indiana." I hadn't intended to say anything further, but it had been a long time since anyone had seen or praised my drawings.

"Oh, how interesting." The man lifted his heavy brows. "Have you come here from Indiana recently?"

"Sorry, I must leave now," I said.

"Please," he said, "Here's my business card. My office is nearby and I was just out for a stroll after lunch."

While I was reading *Jacob Hoffman, Hoffman Imports, 40 La Salle Street, Chicago,* he added, "Might I purchase your drawing? I am collector of art, and I fancy yours greatly."

I was taken aback. *Someone was willing to pay money for my work?* I hadn't even dreamed of that, I was such a beginner still, with as yet no formal art lessons.

144

Who was this man trying to acquaint himself with me on the street? Was he playing a game with me, thinking a young woman sitting alone in public must be a prostitute? On the other hand, what if he were what he said he was, a respectable businessman who is fond of art? It would be foolish to accept money from him, much as I'd like to, but would it hurt to be civil?

"That is kind of you but I'd be happy to make it a gift," I said, rolling my sketch up and handing it to him.

"I am honored," he said, smiling and tucking it under his arm. I noticed he was barely taller than me.

"Well, goodbye, Mr. Hoffman."

"Won't you tell me your name, Miss?"

I hesitated a moment. *Oh, what does it hurt? He doesn't know where I live.* "Victoria Willoughby."

"Miss Willoughby." He tipped his bowler hat. "Please call on me anytime. I would love to talk with you more about your work and art. You might be interested in taking lessons from a very fine artist I know. Clive West."

At that, I fled in a tumult of emotions back to my room at Mrs. Barlow's hat shop.

That March night I had stumbled out of O'Keefe's Tavern, shaking and half-blinded by tears, I paid a dollar for a smelly, sagging cot in a shabby rooming house where I slept fitfully in my clothes, weeping and reliving the miserable scene in the tavern, the way Mama looked and acted and what she said and didn't say. "I hate you," I whispered over and over.

The next morning, I wandered the streets until the comforting thought came to me that while Mama had failed me, I had nearly all of the piano money, enough to rent a room of my own for a while. By this time, I had traveled north to State Street and realized I was out of Conley's Patch and into a better part of Chicago. Instead of taverns, gambling houses, and stables, the street was lined with lawyers' offices, banks, business firms, clothing, and other specialty stores. One of them was a small shop with a sign, Mrs. Barlow's Exclusive Chapeaux for Ladies, above its front window. I stopped, transfixed by the display of colorful, extravagant hats. Some ladies on the train from Shoreside had worn such hats, I recalled. I thought Cousin Abigail would not mind having the gold velvet hat adorned with green ivy and a cluster of purple grapes. She was partial to gold. My

Victoria's Quest

eye fell on a small sign in the corner of the window. *Room to Rent –
Respectable Females Only.* I stepped back on the sidewalk to look up. A
white curtained window peeped above the sign.

Through the window, I saw a stout woman with highly rouged cheeks
dusting a large oval gilt mirror attached to the front of a dressing table. I
entered the shop quickly, pasting on a smile.

"Yes, Madame, may I show you something?" she asked, taking in
my wrinkled dress and bare head.

"I admire your hats very much, but I am here to inquire about the
room to rent. Might you be Mrs. Barlow? I am Miss Willoughby."

"Yes, I am Mrs. Barlow." She put down her dust rag. "You have
perhaps just arrived in Chicago?" she asked, raising her eyebrows.

"Yes, please excuse my appearance. The train was extremely dirty,
and I have not had the time or opportunity to freshen up."

Mrs. Barlow seemed mollified but dubious. "May I ask your purpose
in renting a room? You appear quite young to be unaccompanied."

"I am nearly twenty," I lied. "I look younger than I am. My parents
are gone but my uncle in Indiana has government connections here, having
to do with the War. I have come to do some work for him here."

"I see."

"I could pay you in advance."

Mrs. Barlow adjusted a fold of her dark dress. "I'll show you the
room." I followed her through beige velvet curtains at the back of the
shop into a colorful and chaotic workroom with a sewing machine and
tables of wire and wood hat stands, bolts of fabric, spools of thread, trays of
lace and feathers, rolls of ribbons, and boxes of buttons, sequins, and beads.

We continued up a cramped corner staircase to the second floor.
Behind the closed door immediately next to the stairs were Mrs. Barlow's
private quarters. She walked across the hall and opened the door to another
room, which turned out to belong to the window I had seen above the
shop. The room and everything in it was small – bed, table, chair, dresser
– and I could hear every man's voice and every clatter of horse hooves
from the street below.

"Ten dollars a month," Mrs. Barlow said, "and I expect you to keep
decent hours and entertain no male visitors."

"That is satisfactory," I said, suddenly exhausted and wanting to be alone.

Mrs. Barlow fussed with the curtain at the window until I found my
money in the sack and put it into her hand.

Weekday mornings, I left before 9 o'clock to maintain the charade of going to an office, carrying sketch pad and pencils in a satchel, with the determination to spend my time drawing. If Mrs. Barlow realized there was no uncle or office, she didn't let on. I paid my rent and invited no one, male or female, to my room. With the freedom for a while to do as I wished, I reveled in the excitement of Chicago city life. In the streets, farmers and tradesmen rumbled along in wagons full of squawking chickens, sacks of grain, kegs of beer, and other goods. Ladies and gentlemen peered out from shiny carriages pulled by high-stepping horses. Cowboys on horseback wove in and out among the vehicles. On the sidewalks, men with slicked-back hair in flashy suits muttered and turned from the eyes of passersby to slip bills and coins in one another's hands. Workmen in greasy clothes called rough greetings to one another and sailors wandered by, trailing clouds of whiskey. The few women on the street walked briskly, staring straight ahead and turning quickly into one shop or another. I soon realized, I, too, could not linger on the sidewalk. I hit on the idea of choosing something interesting to draw – a store, a wagon, a man or woman. Then, holding the image as best I could, I ran to a tearoom on Clark Street where I discovered I could stay as long as I liked if I bought a bun and a glass of tea or lemonade. There, I'd sketch from memory. Late in the afternoon, I would return to the hat shop, eat some bread and cheese, and sometimes continue drawing until I could no longer keep my eyes open. Mrs. Barlow was usually in her workroom, for that's when she made new hats and filled orders. On the weekends, she visited her brother and his family who lived west of the city.

The summer was hot and very dry. The cold March when I first arrived, then the heavy April rains were an ancient memory. Like Shoreside, nearly all the structures of Chicago were wood, along with the sidewalks, and it seemed every week something caught on fire. While everyone else was anxious, I was secretly excited when the fire wagons, pulled by enormous draft horses, thundered through the streets to the site of the blaze. If I happened to be anywhere near it, I would draw close, watching burly firemen unwind heavy hoses to spray water on the flames and unhook ladders to climb up to rescue anyone caught inside. Later, I would draw the scene of the fire, always reliving the night of the lightning fire in the lighthouse tower, always trying to recapture the ecstatic feeling of power and fear I'd felt then.

I kept my money under a loose board near the window. I suspected Mrs. Barlow snooped in my room when I was out, but I was equally afraid of being robbed in the street. For weeks, I refused to count what I had left, telling myself I would soon have a job. Every morning I went out with the idea of applying for one, but the prospect of spending my days in dreary, tedious tasks when I wanted only to draw... I'd loiter around shops or small factories with Help Wanted signs in the windows and find myself an hour later once again drawing at my usual tearoom table.

Often, I took out Jacob Hoffman's card in my satchel and rubbed it between my fingers as if it were a paper amulet. How wonderful it would be to take lessons from an art teacher, such as he had suggested! Did I have the courage – or was it foolhardiness – to call on him again? Finally, one very hot day after some hours of unsatisfying drawing and consumption of a cod sandwich I could ill afford, I traveled downtown to LaSalle Street. I walked slowly back and forth in front of his square stone office building, hoping he would come out for his lunchtime walk, which he soon did. A man of regular habits, as I expected.

"Miss Willoughby! How delightful to see you again. How are you?"

"Good afternoon, Mr. Hoffman, I'm fine, thank you," I returned. I had to admit I enjoyed the warm, worldly manner with which he greeted me.

He began talking very fast. "You know I liked your picture so much, I've had it framed and hung in my office. Would you like to come upstairs and see it?"

"Oh, my," I said. Unable to resist this flattery, I agreed to follow him. Still, I was relieved when he left his office door open to an outer reception area occupied by a clerk, nose-deep in a stack of accounts.

"I put this opposite my desk so I can look at it every day," Mr. Hoffman beamed, pointing to the sketch, ridiculously glorified in an ornate silver frame.

Laughing a little, I turned my attention to the oil painting of a plump woman with meek eyes in a pink gown on another wall. Mr. Hoffman followed my gaze. "Clive West, you recall the art teacher I told you about?"

"Yes."

"He painted this of my late wife, Hildegarde."

"Oh, I see. It's a fine painting." My words were sincere. I didn't know what Hildegarde Hoffman had looked like in real life, but the painting technique was skilled and expressive.

"Clive is excellent, isn't he?" He took a step closer to me. "Why don't we discuss him further over a glass of iced tea at The Willows. It's only a few blocks away. A lady is perfectly safe in a hotel dining room."

He offered his arm with an encouraging smile and a slight bow. I hesitated, then laid my hand lightly on his sleeve.

The Willows was a handsome brick, six-story hotel, with fountains and marble statues in the lobby. At a white-clothed table in the dining room, we drank chilled tea in tall crystal glasses. I also ate as many of the sweet tiny iced cakes as I dared, four or five, which seemed to amuse Mr. Hoffman.

He talked while I ate, not about art but himself. He mentioned again he was a widower and also that he had no children. He said he had distracted himself from grief and loneliness by working very hard. He felt fortunate to be able to afford a large home along the lake, which was much cooler in the summer.

"That would be very pleasant," I agreed, thinking of the airless furnace I slept in at Mrs. Barlow's. "Have you been in business in Chicago long?"

"Oh, about five years now, I think, shortly before the War. I import goods from New York to Chicago. Unfortunate as it is, the War has proved very profitable for me." He shook his head as if he had no control over the situation. "I am pro-Union, of course, and employ a freed Negro as my coachman," he added, which gladdened me. I would not have liked him to be against the freedom of Negroes like Sadie and her family.

"Do you think the War will end soon?" I asked.

"I hear rumors it will, but the South hasn't given up yet." Jacob changed the subject. "But now you must tell me something about yourself, Miss Willoughby. How long have you been in Chicago?"

"Several months."

"Your family is in Indiana, I recall."

"Yes, I'm on my own."

He leaned across the table and looked me straight in the eye. "As good as you already are, Miss Willoughby, I know you'd become very, very good if you had lessons from Clive West."

"Yes, but I don't have the means at present," I blurted.

"That does not have to be a problem," Mr. Hoffman said.

"We'd have to make some decent arrangement," I said nervously.

"Yes, that's true. You move into my house – I have plenty of rooms and can turn one of them into a studio for you – and learn to paint portraits and I'll sell them." He threw his head back and laughed, revealing a gold tooth near the back of his mouth.

"Oh." I knew that was no decent arrangement at all. No better, maybe even worse, than Mama's life, playing piano at O'Keefe's in exchange for – what? – I didn't want to know.

"Well, think about it, Miss Willoughby. It's a standing offer," Mr. Hoffman said confidently. "Look, I'll write my home address on the back of my card in case you want to reach me outside business hours."

With that, we parted, and all the way back to Mrs. Barlow's, I had an image of Mr. Hoffman as a practical farmer dangling carrots in front of me, a skittish mare, to lure me into the barn. I was ashamed I had not rejected the proposition at once.

But, then, I became ill, I believe it must have been food poisoning of some sort. I stayed in my room for over a week. Mrs. Barlow called a doctor, who said I was young and strong and would be well soon. His fee ate up nearly all the rest of my money, but I was too listless to care. One windy warm Saturday morning in August, desperate for some fresh air, I forced myself out of bed. Mrs. Barlow had gone to visit her brother as usual for the day. Ignoring my dizziness, I dressed and went out to the tearoom. Fuzzy headed and coughing, I drew an old woman in a black cape I'd seen on the street. Within an hour, I left to go back to my room, feeling weak and feverish again. On the way, two fire wagons passed me and I saw not far ahead, in the direction of the hat shop, a dark cloud of billowy smoke. In a panic, I hurried that way, stopping every few steps to cough and get my balance. Firemen were shouting and swarming around the hat shop when I turned onto State Street. I swooned at the sight of flames shooting from my upstairs window. The whole building was ablaze and the air stank of burning cloth and feathers. I staggered, clung to a lamp post and then sank to the sidewalk, soiling my skirt in the muddy water running down the street. I sat there, unseeing, I don't know how long. All the work I had done, all the drawings and sketches, were burned up as surely as if Papa had stuffed them in the lighthouse stove. The little money I had was gone, everything was gone.

When the flames were finally out and the onlookers drifted away, I got up and went over to a fireman mopping black soot from his sweaty face.

"Mrs. Barlow – she owns the hat shop – is away at her brother's. I rented a room from her. That one." I pointed to the blackened frame of the upstairs front window.

"That's good, then. She's safe and you're safe. We didn't find anyone inside but you never know." He inspected a burn on one hand, then looked down at me. "Do you have somewhere to go, Miss?"

"Yes," I said slowly, "I guess I do." I took out Mr. Hoffman's card and turned it over. "Would you please tell me how to get to this address?"

Dear Joseph,

I woke early this morning after a night of bad dreams, or so I assumed from the glimpse of menacing figures slipping out of memory's reach as soon as I opened my eyes. I felt a brief moment of satisfaction recalling yesterday's bold move to ensure Sister Margaret's help. This was followed by a long moment of dread that something would go wrong with my plan. Sister Margaret was not at breakfast, and I was further alarmed when Sister Winifred laid a timid hand on my arm at the door of my room.

"Mother Superior would like to see you, at your convenience, in the next half hour, Victoria," she said, her voice so low it was hard to hear the words.

"Is Sister Margaret well?" I exclaimed.

Sister Winifred stepped back, startled. "I believe so." Her eyes blinked rapidly. "Shall I say you'll be there shortly?"

"Yes. Thank you, Sister."

In my room, I sat on the bed a few minutes, eyes closed, taking deep breaths that I hoped would calm me but instead made my head dizzy. Or maybe it was only my thoughts – *had Sister Margaret already gone to Mother Superior with some lie about me so Mother Superior wouldn't believe me if I made good my threat? Would she force me to leave St. Mary's Haven before I gave birth?* Finally, reluctantly, I got up and made my unsteady way down the hall and up the stairs. The upstairs hall was silent, all the teaching nuns off at school. I tapped on her office door and Mother Superior commanded, "Come in, Victoria," as if she could see me through it.

She was seated at her desk, pen in hand, reading a file of papers. I had only seen the desk open once, the day I arrived at St. Mary's Haven. It was closed all the time I was painting Dennis' portrait. It was a shock to see the pigeonholes stuffed with envelopes and papers covering the desk top, spilling out the secret life of the home.

"You may sit there," she said, motioning me to the sturdy wooden chair Dennis had posed in. There was still a faint odor of paint in the air.

"So," she said, rhythmically tapping the top paper with her pen. I saw my name and realized it was my file she was looking at. "You've been at St. Mary's Haven almost three months."

"Yes, quite so, Reverend Mother." My head was still spinning in crackles of light.

"And what do you think of your experience?" she demanded.

"I'm grateful – very grateful – to be here."

"You have maintained your health? Sister Margaret reports no problems."

"Quite well, yes." I had told no one of my bleeding and stomach pain.

"Even to the point of being able recently to paint Mr. Kelly's portrait, I see. It was rather novel for my office to be a temporary art studio," Mother Superior said drily.

I cleared my throat. "I was honored to have the opportunity. Mr. Kelly is very pleasant."

"Indeed."

"And Sister Margaret so kind."

Mother Superior looked up. "Oh?"

"The way she has taken care of Jean."

"Jean, poor girl, yes." Mother Superior sighed.

"Thanks to the charity of St. Mary's Haven, Jean has a good future now," I chattered on, smiling and nodding.

"Charity is a charge from God to all the sisters, to every one of us."

"Christian charity," I murmured, clasping my hands tightly across my stomach and feeling Mother Superior gathering energy for what she would say next. She frowned and leaned toward me.

"I am very much hoping you will return to the Catholic Church. As you told me when you arrived, your mother is Catholic and you are already baptized."

So this is what she wanted! I felt faint with relief. I paused before answering, thinking, *Mama may be Catholic but she is more sinful than any woman here.* "I shall consider it seriously." My face burned in shame at the flush of pleasure in the face opposite me.

"I can arrange for you to meet with Father Gerald and discuss it." Mother Superior looked poised to clap her hands.

"Thank you, Reverend Mother." *Did she make this request of all the girls,* I wondered, *hoping for converts like Jean?* If that didn't work, perhaps she made a final attempt when we were in labor and helpless to refuse.

Mother Superior leaned back as if she had dispensed with the most important business. "I will also secure a household position for you to go to when you leave us."

I allowed myself a small laugh. "Thank you, but I won't be staying in Chicago. Elise and I are going to Philadelphia together."

"Elise is a woman of means, I understand. I'm sure you feel fortunate." She gave me a curious look and then closed my file. "I hope all goes well with you, Victoria. I won't keep you any longer this morning. God be with you. Father Gerald will contact you soon."

Dismissed but still agitated from this encounter, I went straight to Elise's room. She, too, was sitting at a table with pen and paper. "Ah, Victoria, I've just finished writing to Aunt and Uncle that I shall arrive with a female companion in approximately six weeks' time and that I shall send a telegram when we begin our journey."

I leaned down to give her a quick hug, breathing in her usual scent of roses. "Elise, tell me our dreams are going to come true, our dreams of fame and accomplishment."

"Of course, they will," she said, signing her name with a flourish. "As soon as this is over with, it's on to a new life." She folded the letter and slid it smoothly into an envelope.

I sank down on her bed and looked around the room. While it was furnished as drably as the rest, she had made it almost stylish with her pink silk coverlet over the standard gray blanket, lace doily on the dresser, and silver-backed brush and comb set on the shelf above the washstand. An image of my room in Jacob's house flitted by. "I am more than ready to have this baby," I declared, rubbing a hand across the soft pink cloth.

"Me, too!"

"When my time comes, I'm going to give Sister Margaret my bracelet for the baby," I added, watching her address and stamp the envelope in swift, graceful motions.

"That's a sentimental idea." Elise turned and widened her eyes.

"Do I appear that unfeeling?" *Perhaps I had put on my blank look too many times even with Elise.*

"No, I didn't mean that, Victoria," she said quickly. "I was only thinking for myself I have thought it best my baby have no connection or memory of me. Best for him and the woman who raises him."

"It's selfish of me, but I still want to do it."

"But I know our situations are different," Elise said softly. "I had no control over what happened and yours is a...love child."

"Still, the consequences unfairly punish both of us, don't they?"

"Yes, and I refuse to keep paying for a crime I did not commit," Elise declared.

"We'll be out of prison soon," I joked, and returned to my room.

Victoria's Quest

Once there, I sat at my own table with a fresh page of the log. Some might call me a criminal to blackmail the Kellys but I didn't care. Painting a portrait was what I had to do to safeguard my daughter's future, just as it was in Jacob's house to ensure my own as an artist.

Portraits
(Chicago, August 1863-September 1865)

Jacob Hoffman's immense brick mansion faced Lake Michigan north of the Chicago River. I did not reach it until late afternoon. Close to fainting both from my illness and my long walk through the steaming city, I leaned my hand on the front door and let a breeze from the lake cool me a moment before I knocked. A young maid answered and flicked suspicious eyes over my grimy face and clothes. "No handouts here," she said, shutting the door at once. I retreated wearily down the front walk and slumped to the grass to lean against the brick entrance pillars and stare at the water. From this distance, the lake and the sky melted into a single soothing haze of blue. In my exhaustion, I dozed a while until roused by the rattle of carriage wheels and horse hoofs. I looked up to see a slope-shouldered Negro behind a pair of bays draw a glossy black carriage up the driveway next to the mansion. I hastened to my feet, light-headed, and stumbled after them.

"Sam, be sure to cool the horses a good while." Jacob bounced down the carriage step.

"Yes, Sir." The Negro, who had deep creases in his face, slapped the reins across the horses' backs and urged them toward a cavernous open carriage house at the end of the driveway. Jacob turned and saw me. "Miss Willoughby!" he exclaimed. He was shorter and stouter than I remembered.

My words tumbled out. "A fire burned down the hat shop and everything I have and I'm ill..."

He stopped me with a raised hand. "It's all right. Welcome to my home." He ushered me in the side door to a dark parlor with brocade chairs. "Wait here a moment while I make arrangements." He went out and came back with the maid who had turned me away. "This is Caroline," he said.

"Ma'am." The maid's eyes darted past me.

Jacob didn't notice. "She'll show you to your room. If you feel well enough, please join me for dinner."

"Thank you." I said weakly, my relief at his immediate welcome emptying the breath from my throat.

Gripping the carved banister with each step, I followed Caroline up the wide central hall staircase to the second floor. The maid flung a pointed finger at a closed door on the right, saying – "Mr. Hoffman's room" – and continued walking. Farther down the hall, she opened another door, saying, "I'm sorry if I was rude. I didn't know you were a friend of Mr. Hoffman's." It was an accusation more than an apology.

"Certainly. You couldn't have," I said absently, drinking in the sight of a large ruffled canopy bed of white painted wood with matching wardrobe, bureau, and mirrored dressing table, a flowered carpet, and a bay window with a clear view of the lake. *This was how I had once imagined life with Mama!*

The maid went out and returned shortly with a stack of white towels and a china pitcher of fresh water which she set on the bureau. After she left, I lay on the thick coverlet and stared up at the underside of the canopy, knowing without looking in the mirror that my face wore its familiar blank look. I would not allow myself to feel yet the shame of what I had done, that I was willing to trade my body for shelter and food rather than give up art and take a job to earn my keep.

After a while, I got up and washed my face and hands. Feeling slightly better, I made my way downstairs and found the dining room, which looked nearly twice as large and elaborately furnished as Cousin Abigail's. *What I wouldn't give for her to see me now,* I thought. Jacob was seated at one end of a long polished mahogany table. He stood up when I walked in.

"Ah, Victoria. Your food's still warm, I believe." He indicated a covered dish at the other end of the table. "Do you find your room comfortable?" He spoke as heartily as Cousin Sherman inquiring about my school day those many years past, and I wondered briefly if I was mistaken, that Jacob Hoffman had something quite innocent in mind after all.

"It's lovely, thank you."

"I'm drinking wine, but there's iced tea for you. I thought that would suit you better until you're completely well. Please, sit down."

Victoria's Quest

"I'm afraid I can't eat very much this evening," I apologized, removing the silver lid to find a plateful of steak, potatoes, corn, and summer squash.

"Just take what you can. You must build up your strength." He sipped his wine and asked for details of the fire, which I gave between small forkfuls of the vegetables. "I hope Mrs. Barlow will be able to re-open her hat shop," I concluded, though in my heart I was quite indifferent.

Jacob lifted his glass. "I'm so glad you are here, Victoria. A toast to the artist. You have a great future."

"You are most encouraging, Mr. Hoffman," I said, venturing to cut into the steak.

"Jacob, please, please," he protested, finishing a swallow of wine. "I didn't have a chance to tell you during our delightful tea at The Willows. One of my greatest pleasures is giving a helping hand to promising young people."

"How very generous." I took a bite of peppery beef that, while deliciously tender, caused my stomach to churn and my face to perspire.

Jacob shifted in his chair, and his tone sharpened slightly. "Have you drawn human faces, Victoria?"

"Some," I said, dabbing at my forehead with a napkin. "More like sketches."

"Well, I feel sure you can master the technique of formal portraiture. It's very popular these days among my business friends and acquaintances to commission a portrait of themselves and members of their families. Clive West does quite well at it and, as I mentioned, he's a fine teacher, a graduate of a Pennsylvania art academy."

I forgot my queasiness for a moment. *At last, the chance to learn from a trained artist! Wasn't this what I had dreamed of through those recess hours in Mr. Briscoe's classroom, those dark evenings in my attic room at Cousin Abigail's?* "I'd be most interested, Mr... Jacob," I breathed.

"Good, very good." Jacob leaned back and laced his fingers across his chest. I suspected this was his habit at the completion of a business transaction.

"I'm glad to know I will be able to earn a living from my art, that I won't impose on your kindness for long." To remove the proposal from the personal, I added, "My work can bring a good return on your investment."

Jacob sat up and frowned at me down the table. "Let's talk about all that later. You know, Victoria, you are looking quite pale." Despite the concern of his words, his voice sounded almost harsh.

Suddenly, the rich meat backed up in my throat. "Forgive me, I'm feeling ill again," I cried, upsetting my plate in my haste to get up.

"Of course, I'll help you back upstairs and call a doctor," Jacob said. "You mustn't worry about anything from now on."

Over the next few days, the doctor having decided I was only in need of bed rest and nourishing food, Caroline silently delivered meals on a tray to my room and I tried to think of nothing but my good fortune. Jacob waved away my further attempts to discuss a financial arrangement, distracting me with the news that a studio was being set up for me from an unused storage room on the third floor. I told myself he only wanted to be sure my work was going to be good enough to sell before we made any agreement. If not, he would feel free to ask me to leave and count it as a loss. The thought frightened me into silence. I didn't want to jeopardize my future before it started!

Three days later, Clive West arrived with oil painting supplies and a disdainful manner. He was a tall, sleepy-eyed man somewhere in his thirties.

"So you fancy being a woman artist," he said, setting down tubes of paint, brushes, and a palette on the studio table. At present, the room held only the table, two chairs, an easel, and a folding screen for a backdrop. The window, to my disappointment, faced west into the city rather than out to the lake.

"Yes," I said, ignoring the insulting tone. "I look forward to learning everything I can from you."

He smiled thinly but proceeded to do just that over the next several weeks. He taught me to stretch canvas on wooden frames and adjust the easel to my height and the light of the day. He taught me the magic of mixing the bright dabs of reds, blues, yellows, whites and blacks on my palette into endless magical shades of colors. He taught me to clean brushes – I immediately loved the smell of turpentine. He taught me to start the drawing of a head with an egg shape; to use flattened curves for the eyelids; circles for the iris and pupil; four lines to outline the upper lip ("it looks like a pair of wings") and three lines for the lower lip. He taught me to figure the width of one eye as the space for the nose between the eyes and for the base of the nose and likewise two eyes' width for the mouth, and to align the ears with the nose and eyes. He taught me how to draw hair, necks, chests, and hands and how to shadow the face according to the direction of the light. All these techniques led to the creation of a realistic portrait but for all I was learning, I missed the spontaneity of drawing what I wished, of letting my hand move as it would.

During this time, Jacob was out of town a great deal, traveling to New York and Boston on business. He acted as if I were only a roomer in the house, to my relief, and we generally met only at dinner, where he talked about what he'd seen on his trips, including reports of the War in that part of the country, and I offered details of my lessons.

Then, Clive said I was ready to paint my first portrait. "It shall be of me, of course," Jacob declared. After he settled into the chair before me, in a sudden inspiration I pinned a map of downtown Chicago on the folding screen as a backdrop. The hours of his posing and my work passed in a blur of nerves. What if I did not have the talent to paint a decent portrait? But when it was finished, I thought it a fair likeness of my subject, though Clive merely nodded, expressionless. Jacob, however, was pleased. "Just what I was hoping for!" he exclaimed.

He immediately arranged for my second portrait, the wife of one of his business associates. "I've signed the contract, you don't need to do anything but paint," he said. "What fee will I be paid," I dared to ask. "Oh, I thought you understood your fees for a good while will go to me for, as you said, the investment."

That night, near midnight, as I was finally easing into a troubled sleep, I heard my bedroom door open and my benefactor appeared in a dressing gown. He crossed the room, pulled back the coverlet, and got into my bed, flooding it with the smell of wine, hair tonic, and salty perspiration. "You knew this would happen, sooner or later, didn't you, Victoria?" He pulled me next to his coarse skin and hairy body. I nearly gagged in revulsion.

"Are you cold, dear?" he breathed in my ear as I tried to still my shivering body.

"A little." I willed my body to relax. Then, with a final shudder, I accepted my bargain with the devil. Art was all I wanted to do, what gave meaning to my life. Jacob was making it possible and I was at his mercy.

Over the next year, I painted pale women with petulant smiles in ornate gowns and jewelry, ruddy men in high collars and heavy suits, flushed children in lace dresses or velvet jackets. My signature was to place an item in the hand of the sitter – an opera ticket, a ball invitation, a menu, a business report, a doll or a toy soldier. My subjects seemed happy with the results and asked me no personal questions, probably at Jacob's request. After a while, Jacob gave me a portion of the commissions, but the money went only for painting supplies and my wardrobe. He liked me to be dressed fashionably at dinner, though we ate alone. For his business, he preferred to play the host at hotels like The Willows instead of entertain at home.

As the months turned into a year, I felt as imprisoned as if I were back at Shoreside Light. I remembered with longing my freedom at Mrs. Barlow's, of sketching whatever caught my imagination of street scenes and ordinary people.

One night the ghost returned, the first time it had appeared other than at the lighthouse. It howled its way down the chimney from the top floor and rattled the panes of the bay window as I lay sweating and trembling in my black lace nightgown.

The War ended in April of 1865, and the news increased my restlessness, that I, too, had to find some kind of peace. In the summer, I began to go out by myself on foot an hour or two between sittings to make sketches. The first day I went back to the bench where I had met Jacob and drew another lake sketch but with no joy. That night, listening to the slapping of waves at the bay window, I fancied the lake's spray misting my face, its scent in my nostrils, and felt a terrible sadness I couldn't explain even to myself.

From then on, I traveled the streets, searching out other subjects to draw and stopping in a hotel tearoom to sketch them. One hot morning, I wandered into some poorer streets filled with Negroes and realized this might be where Sadie Fry had come with her family. *How I would love to see her again! What kind of young woman had she become? What had happened in her life since she had passed through the Fogartys' house?* As a white woman, I didn't feel comfortable seeking her out myself, but when I returned to the mansion I asked Sam to inquire for me and set aside a little of my allowance as a reward if he was successful.

Caroline must have told Jacob I often left the mansion alone in the daytime. At the front door one morning, he kissed me, clamping my head tightly between his hands.

"Why do you go out so much when I'm not home, Victoria?" he muttered when he released me. "Are you going to meet some man?"

I rubbed the sides of my face. "No, Jacob, of course not." My smile was forced. "I only go out to sketch as I used to."

He looked at me suspiciously. "Well, you don't have time now. You have portraits to paint and it's not respectable to wander the streets." His voice got louder with each sentence.

"The day you met me, I was outdoors drawing," I tried to remind him. "You seemed very happy with my lake sketch."

"Means to an end. You're under my roof. You'll do what I say." He bit off the words and slammed the door.

Jacob's anger was frightening. I told myself I dared not go out alone for a long time, which only made me more desperate to do so. A week later, I found myself canceling a scheduled sitting and sneaking out the side door.

On the street where I was walking, gathering images to draw, a shoe store had caught fire just as a farmer with a wagon of vegetables was passing. Maddened by the bright flames and heat and smell of burning leather, the farmer's black mare bolted and broke into a gallop. Barely realizing what I was doing, I kept pace on the sidewalk with the runaway, staring at her frantic legs, rippling flanks, tossing head, and wild eyes. The farmer shouted and whipped and pulled the reins to slow the horse until finally, two streets later, she stopped dead, her head hanging and sides heaving. I was out of breath myself and so stirred by the sight I could not settle to drawing what I'd seen.

Returning to the mansion, I discovered Jacob had come home early. When he saw my disheveled hair, mud-splattered dress, and sketchbook, he went into a rage.

"You're mine and you will obey me," he shouted, slapping me hard across the face.

Very late that night, when I was sure he was asleep, I sat on my bed with my sketchbook, my swollen cheeks still stinging, filling one page after another with my vision of that horse in its panic and its glory, straining endlessly forward and free.

Entry 22 -- 11 Apr. 1868 – Weather: overcast, rainy

Dear Joseph,

The hours before I give birth are slipping away as fast as the last sinking of sand through the neck of an hourglass – for this part of my life, that is. The next part in Philadelphia promises to be so glorious I wonder how much I will even remember of this painful interlude at St. Mary's Haven and of what I have written in this log.

Sister Margaret pretends I am invisible whenever we pass in the hall or meet in the dining hall. She moves like an old woman and her limp seems worse, though that may be only my guilty imagining.

After lunch today, as I was resting, Dennis walked into my room without knocking and stood over me with a clenched fist. "Victoria! How dare you talk to my sister that way!" he stormed.

Keeping my eyes on his angry face, I slowly got to my feet. "We can't talk here. The walls have ears, Dennis," I said calmly, though I was quite unnerved.

We stared at each other, and then he let his hand drop. "Very well. We'll take a walk outdoors."

"I can manage only a short distance," I warned.

"As a gentleman, I should excuse you from the exertion of walking in your present condition, but I won't," he said, marching ahead of me to the front door.

❈

Outside, our umbrellas served as shields against the gusting wind, the blowing drizzle – and each other.

As soon as we got to the sidewalk, Dennis lashed out. "I consider myself a good judge of character, but I failed miserably in assessing yours."

"You refer, I assume, to the character judgment of adoptive parents? That's just what I question – your right to judge, to decide." I tilted my umbrella to hide the anxiety in my face that belied my blunt words.

165

Victoria's Quest

He recited his answer like a solemn speech, staring straight ahead and walking so fast I fell some steps behind. "I'm a teaching Brother. I know all the parents. I know which ones are raising fine Catholic boys. They know worthy childless fellow Catholics eager to take in a baby. They know of my mission and they tell me. I am ideally qualified to do the work Mother Superior charges me to do."

"Oh, I do doubt that, Dennis," I said, catching up. "If they knew the choices, the girls are perfectly capable of deciding which home their baby should go."

"Utter chaos," he protested, tightening the grip on his umbrella handle. "Such decisions should not be in the hands of fallen women who are not well in either body or mind."

"Then you force me to tell the truth about your sister." The wind shifted, and the spattering rain soaked my skirt.

He glared at me. "What do you mean?"

"Pretending ignorance is no use," I said quietly. "I know in Sister Margaret's past is the same experience the rest of us are undergoing. But as I told her, I will keep her secret from Mother Superior. It should be no one's business but her own just as it should be for all the girls here once we leave. All I ask, all I beg, is that the two of you take my newborn to the family I wish."

After my words, he was silent for several paces. We came to the end of the street. I turned around, with him reluctantly following, the wind now at our backs. Then he seized my arm and I felt fury in the press of his fingers. "Margaret has had a very hard life. She didn't deserve what happened to her. She continues to punish herself much too harshly."

I jerked my arm from his grasp, nearly losing my balance, and felt my own anger rise. My words tumbled out recklessly. "Most women have hard lives. We don't have men's weapons of strength and money. We must use other means to survive and get what we want, which often means deceiving – or depending on men. In fact you yourself, I think, know the reward of being cosseted by a man."

Dennis stopped dead, his face a mask of rage. "You are a devil and I curse the day you arrived at St. Mary's Haven."

"Demons drive us all, I've learned." I was amazed at the neutral tone of my own voice. *What an unbridled state of mind I had reached.*

"Blackmail," he said suddenly. "That's why you wanted to paint my portrait."

"That was not all, truly," I said, knowing he wouldn't believe me. "I came alive again as an artist, painting your picture. I am grateful for that."

"How nice," he said, curling his lip. "Now every time Margaret looks at the portrait, she sees only your betrayal."

"Or maybe she just doesn't want to know the truth about you anymore than she wants the world – or Mother Superior – to know the truth about her."

We had reached the steps of the home.

"You are going to hell, Victoria." Dennis viciously shook the rain from his umbrella.

"Aren't you?" I asked, collapsing my umbrella carefully and then opening the door, waiting.

There was a long pause.

At last, Dennis said, "We will take your child where you ask," and stomped away.

Back in my room, I pulled off my wet dress and burrowed gratefully under the blankets of my bed. I lay there, my legs twitching and my breath coming in gasps from the exertion of the walk while the baby in my stomach shifted and kicked as if telling me she understood her fate was settled. Though others may not see it as such, I had triumphed over the adversary. I had won over Dennis, just as I had won over Jacob when I defied him once and for all. As it is now, so it was then a time of regaining control of my future.

Later... it occurs to me that it was Sadie Fry who made possible both victories, past and present. I have regained enough strength to sit at my desk and record in the log those fateful meetings with her amid my misery with Jacob.

Sadie
(Chicago, September - October 1865)

The following morning, Jacob apologized, his eyes glistening with tears, for hitting me. "I didn't mean to hurt you, dear Victoria, I'm sorry. I was angry that you'd been so reckless, for your sake. It seemed the only way to bring you to your senses."

"Perhaps I should leave," I said, the thought of it immediately lifting my heart.

"Well, now, that's not very grateful," Jacob said quickly. "You do still owe me a fair amount for art lessons and room and board."

"I'll never get out of debt to you unless I get more of the portrait commission fees," I protested.

"You have talent, Victoria, but you're still an apprentice and should earn an apprentice's salary," Jacob said.

Defeated, I turned away, thinking, *an indentured servant is what I am.* I had asked the last client to pay me directly but he said Jacob had made it clear he was the proper agent for my work, that I was not to have anything to do with money.

From then on, I was nothing but an actress, as if I were trading lines on stage with the other characters. Every day, I smiled and chatted with my clients. Every night, I appeared to eat the food on my plate while becoming adept at mashing most of it into tiny mounds with my fork and answering Jacob's questions about how I spent my day. He even checked my easel now and then to make sure I was working on the portrait I said I was. What a price I was paying to be an artist, accepting Jacob's supporting me and losing my freedom. The ghost mocked me in the night with the face of the devil.

"I found your Sadie Fry, Miss," Sam called from the driveway one afternoon in October. At the front gate, I had just waved off in her carriage fussy, elderly Mrs. Porter after a painting session.

"Oh, I'm glad. Thank you." I walked to where he was hitching the bays, Lilly and Marigold, to Jacob's carriage. In the fall sunshine, their bodies gleamed from Sam's faithful brushing.

"She sure was excited when I asked her your question, was she the Sadie that had her drawing done by Victoria," he said, patting the nose of the nearest horse, Marigold.

"I couldn't be sure she'd remember." I was pleased.

"Sadie says, can you meet her at the corner of State and Randolph a week from today. Around two o'clock?"

"Please tell her yes, Sam. If I can't get away, though, I'll have to send you to let her know."

"As you wish, Miss," Sam said, pressing a finger into a crease along his mouth.

"I'll have your reward ready when you return, Sam."

He nodded. "'Preciate it, Miss."

Fortunately, the following Saturday Jacob went to an all-day business meeting on the south side of Chicago where the new stockyards had opened. I dressed with care, choosing a favorite dress of deep green and a purple cape with a jeweled clasp.

The steady-eyed Sadie wearing a trim, high-necked blue dress and black shawl who met me at the appointed time bore little resemblance to the frightened little girl in rags of yesteryear. She had grown at least a head taller than me and become statuesque, her girlish boniness transformed by both height and weight.

She seemed as astonished by my appearance. "Miss Victoria, is that you?" she exclaimed. "You look rich!" She stopped and put a hand to her mouth. "Oh, I didn't mean to be forward, please excuse me."

I laughed. "Sadie, I remember saying you were the princess granddaughter of an African king. Now I know I was right!"

"I didn't know you even remembered me."

"Of course, I did. That scared, brave little girl who let me draw her picture."

"I thought you had magical powers the way you did that!"

We grinned at each other and I think she felt as gladdened as I did at our common link to the past. "Let's walk a while," I suggested. "Isn't Chicago an exciting place to live? I never get tired of looking at everything."

"I'm still not used to the cold winters." Her face opened in her radiant smile.

We strolled, silently admiring pretty items in the store windows as we talked.

"You must be very happy – I am, too, of course – that the War is over. What are you doing now, Sadie?"

"Well, soon after my Daddy's brother – Uncle Ralph – took me in his family, we all moved to Chicago. Good jobs for Negroes here." As she spoke, I studied her face, mixing imaginary paint on my palette, puzzling out a combination of browns and yellows and reds to match the beautiful sienna of her skin.

Sadie held out her hand to show me a ring. "I got married to a wonderful man. George Wingate. He works for Jarvis. That's the biggest grain elevator in Chicago," she said proudly. "We're hoping to have children soon," she added, as if there was doubt.

"And did your father come up North?"

Sadie sighed. "No, he died, still on the plantation."

"I'm so sorry."

"Well, like Miz Fogarty says, it's God who asks us to accept the sorrow and He knows why."

I jumped at the name, guilt constricting my heart.

"Oh, you keep in touch with them?"

"Yes." Sadie lifted her chin high. "I've learned to read and write. I wrote them a letter a while back. Mr. Fogarty wrote back – I mean Miz Fogarty told him what to say."

We both smiled. "Sounds like Uncle Frank and Aunt Maggie, all right," I said. "Is everything well with the family?"

Sadie's smile disappeared. "They lost Anna last year. That's why Miz Fogarty talks about God so much."

"Oh, no!" I groaned and closed my eyes against the news.

"Her little heart gave out," Sadie went on. "Before they buried her someone took her picture in her white christening gown."

"Mr. Briscoe?" I interrupted. I had put out of my mind the memory of his being called occasionally for this sorrowful custom.

Sadie frowned. "Maybe, I don't know who did it."

"It doesn't matter. Go on, then."

"All I was going to say is they said Anna looked like an angel. An angel who's now in heaven."

"Anna *was* an angel," I cried. "Oh, poor Aunt Maggie and Uncle Frank. How can they bear to lose a child!"

Sadie sighed, then hesitated.

"What else can you tell me?" I asked.

"It's not about Anna. It's about your father. The Fogartys wrote something about him."

"What about him?" I asked sharply.

"I expect you know he's a bit poorly."

I nodded as if I did, trying to hide my fear. "Did they see him?"

"Yes, last time he was in town. He was very thin and coughing all the time."

"He's probably been working too hard, but he's a tough old seaman," I said, not believing my own words. *Poor Papa, what has happened to you since I've been gone?*

There was a pause.

"I wonder, are you still drawing, Miss Victoria?"

"Yes, I'm a real artist now. I do portraits of important people."

"You do?" Sadie said. "That's why you're rich, then. You must live in a big house."

"It's big. Near the lake." Reminded of Jacob, I said, "I can't stay much longer today but I'd like to meet again, Sadie. This has been nice."

"That's kind of you," Sadie said cautiously. I knew what she was wondering, could we meet as equals, a white and Negro woman, no matter she was free and the War was over?

"Truly, I would." I patted her arm.

"I still have your drawings," she said, dipping her head.

"Then come to my house, Sadie, and I'll paint your portrait. I'll do it for free, of course."

"Do you want to?" Sadie's voice was eager. "Would it be all right?"

"Yes, I'll find a free morning and work fast," I smiled. "Sam will let you know which day and fetch you." I would have to give him a bit more of my precious store of money.

The following Tuesday, a very cold day, I met Sadie at the back door and told the cook, who was distracted by her semi-annual pantry cleaning, I was getting a delivery of art supplies.

That painting session was the most pleasurable I'd ever had. Sadie wore her blue dress and I posed her holding one graceful hand to her cheek, gazing into the distance with those wide, calm eyes. I brushed on paint quickly, following the lovely lines of her face and features almost without thought or calculation. But I dared not have her stay long or Caroline would surely notice and report to Jacob the oddity of a Negro girl lingering in the studio. I was frustrated that the portrait was going to take a long time to finish.

Then, in early October, Jacob announced he was taking the train to New York City for two days to arrange a large order of goods. I would be free to work on Sadie's portrait. I yearned as well to be free of that prison mansion for a while.

The morning he left, I dressed in my plainest clothes, loaded up the carriage with canvas, easel, and paints, and had Sam drive me to Sadie's. He would fetch me in the late afternoon. Sadie's wood tenement building, one of many lining her street, was noisy and smelled of greasy cooking, but inside her tidy apartment it seemed cool and peaceful. I felt immediately at home. In the front sitting room, where daylight flowed through the window, Sadie shyly showed me the pine table and chairs and upholstered sofa she and George had been able to buy by saving carefully from his pay. I set the canvas on my easel, mixed paints on my palette, and settled her in a pose in a chair.

An hour later, as I was putting some finishing touches to her face, the contours of her high cheekbones and sweet smile of her full lips, we both jumped at the loud knock at the door.

Sadie went to open it and led the caller back to the front room. He was a short, handsome young Negro with sharp eyes and a confident walk.

"Victoria, this is George's brother, Joseph."

(Do you recall that moment, Joseph, as plainly as I do?)

"Joseph, Victoria is from Indiana where a family took me in on my way up North. She found me a few weeks ago."

"Oh," you said, your face guarded but giving me a relaxed smile. "Pleased to meet you, Miss."

"Hello," I said, liking you at once.

"Victoria's painting my portrait." Sadie pointed to the easel. "It's not done yet. Victoria's working on it all day today."

"I see." You studied the canvas, inclining your head this way and that. "You are painting my sweet sister-in-law's face – and, I believe, capturing her soul."

What an extraordinary thing to say, Joseph! I was stunned.

"Thank you," I said, two inadequate words for the pleasure I felt.

"I speak too boldly about none of my business," you added then. "Please don't pay me mind."

"It's all right," I assured you. "Praise is always welcome to an artist. And please go ahead with your visiting and I'll keep painting."

With a nod, you sat on the sofa opposite Sadie's chair. The two of you talked, but in some sort of code that I surmised had to do with the transport of Negroes from South to North. I accepted that you were not sure I could be trusted, and I concentrated on my painting until I heard you say "a whole new life of freedom." You drew out the word freedom, almost singing it.

"Freedom," I repeated, my hand slipping and brushing a streak across Sadie's chin.

"Yes, that's what I live for," you said. "Bringing people from slavery to freedom."

Your fiery emotion ignited mine. "*I* am a slave!" I erupted, startling you, Sadie, and myself.

"Whatever do you mean, Victoria? You're a free white woman and always have been," Sadie said, breaking her pose.

"It may seem so, but I have enslaved myself in order to be an artist. I may as well be in chains."

"Oh, Victoria. You don't mean that," Sadie said.

"I know now, hearing Joseph talk, that I have to leave where I'm living. I have to leave Chicago."

"Where would you go?"

"Back to my father and the lighthouse."

"That might be good, yes," Sadie said softly.

Then you said, speaking for the first time since my outburst, "Forgive me, Miss, but whatever you do, don't give up your art." Those words I have never forgotten, Joseph, and always blessed you for.

When Sam came for me, I saw a burly white man with a faint smile watch me get into the carriage. I assumed he thought I was a charity worker among the Negroes.

But I was wrong.

"You whore," Jacob snarled when he returned the following day. "I knew I couldn't trust you. I had someone follow you while I was gone." He dropped his veneer of tolerance. "Who are you seeing there. Some slave boy?"

"No one, I mean only an old friend. A girl I once knew in Shoreside."

"I don't believe you," Jacob said, and began to beat me.

The following week, I waited until he had gone to his office and then left the mansion for the last time. Carrying a sack of clothes, Sadie's portrait, and my paints, little more than I had arrived in Chicago with, I walked to the downtown station to board a train to Shoreside.

Entry 23 -- 14 Apr. 1868 – Weather: Bright a.m., storm clouds, thunder

Dear Joseph,

Today I was swept into a frenzy of artistic effort quite like the maelstrom of my last year at Shoreside Light. Was that only some twelve months past? But surely in Philadelphia I will know it again and again, this ecstasy.

It was too great a strain on my burdened body to stand at the easel and balance a palette, so I settled with a sketchbook and pen at my table. Through the day, I shifted my body constantly to ease discomfort but did not lift my pen unless my wrist prickled with pain, my hand numbed, or my fingers stiffened.

As for the subjects, I began with this room – the bed, desk, washstand, and window that document the world in which I have lived these past months. In Philadelphia, I am sure my memory of it will be lost in the sights and surroundings of my new life.

Then, the St. Mary's Haven sisters – Sister Barbara with a pan of (burned) biscuits, Sister Rosamund with a sewing basket, Mother Superior with papers at her desk, and yes, Sister Margaret, whom I drew holding a letter whose contents could not be read. At intervals I would lie down, overcome with fatigue, but then was driven to return to the table and continue.

Sister Barbara ringing the lunch bell shocked me back to the present. In a fog, I made my way to the dining hall. I nibbled at soup and bread, saying little and not even knowing what my mouth was saying, staring at my companions on this journey who, except for Elise, I will never see again.

Returning to my room, I hurried to sketch their faces – Jean, Emma, Jane, Alice. I had only to fix a stare to have them appear like an hallucinatory dream, one after another, in the space beyond my table. Through the afternoon, I burned one candle after another to augment the poor light from the overcast day outside my window. I smiled every time I lit a fresh candle, remembering how many I used of Cousin Abigail's. I bear no malice toward her now as I truly hope she no longer bears me.

Victoria's Quest

Finally, finally, I drew you, Joseph, the best and finest and sweetest. I had only to close my eyes an instant for your image to burn on the inside of my lids like a photographic negative. Yes, I have drawn your face many times, but I wanted the pleasure of bringing your beloved face to life beneath my fingers one more time. I will put that drawing in the package with the bracelet and the log.

When I was finished, I was stunned to see on the floor next to the table the tall stack of sketches I had done. I laid down on my bed, rubbing the aches from my fingers and hands and listening to the rumbling thunder. I was too spent to respond to the dinner bell.

Some time later, I opened my eyes to see Elise leaning over me. "Are you all right? Have your pains come on?"

"No, not yet. I am only very tired."

"You must eat." She went out and returned with a dinner tray from Sister Barbara. She kept me company while I picked at the food. As soon as I was finished, I closed my eyes. "Thank you, Elise, I'm much better now. I need to rest."

But I could not sleep after she left. I summoned the will to write of this extraordinary day and of the recent events that brought me to you, Joseph, and this fate.

Papa
(October 1865 - April 1866)

On the train ride to Shoreside, I kept my face turned toward the window to hide my tears and spoke to no one. Only two years ago, I had traveled in the opposite direction toward Chicago, full of excitement, certain that my reunion with Mama would be the beginning of my glorious career as an artist. And then the bitter disappointment of finding her in O'Keefe's Tavern, of being alone again, of letting the money I had slip away over the next months, and of trading my freedom and morals for a place to live and the chance to continue as an artist. I had learned a bitter truth in Chicago: It was impossible to be an independent woman and an artist without my own income. And I could not earn it if I was consumed with the work of drawing and painting. What difference had my efforts made? My dreams had come to nothing except experience in making sketches and painting oil portraits. Now I was back where I had begun with little hope for the future. Papa was ill and needed me. I needed a place to live and to recover from the humiliating life I had fallen into. After the fire at the hat shop, I had no other choice than to go to Jacob. Now, I had no other place to go but to the lighthouse.

When I arrived at the station and walked through town, the bustling activity of the streets and the new stores and houses told me Shoreside, like Chicago, had prospered during the War. Though it was early afternoon and I needed quickly to find someone at the harbor willing to take me out to the island, I hurried through the cold chill of the morning to the cemetery. Jacob had often talked about the War at dinner and I had said little in return, for the subject reminded me painfully of Paul's death. Now I found a brief comfort sitting next to his grave a while, running my fingers over his carved name while leaves drifted to the ground around me. I pictured his laughing, young face and felt the years lengthen between us as if between an entire generation, the memory of our past together fond, but distant. At least he'd been spared the horror of being a prisoner at a place like Camp Douglas. Wherever he was now, he was free, on foot or on horseback, eagerly heading toward a new adventure.

I got up and wandered the paths until I found another grave with a new small headstone adorned with a lamb and the words, "Anna, our beloved baby, gone to rest, February 1864." Again, I sank to the ground and with fresher sorrow. The air and my breath seemed to stop moving at the same time. I wrapped my arms around my knees and swayed back and forth, as if I were once more rocking that small, frail girl in the Fogartys' kitchen.

The big strong Papa I had looked up to was no more. In his place was a stooped man with mild eyes and slow steps.

"I had given you up for dead, girl!" he wheezed in ragged breaths when I arrived with my belongings at midday. The boatman who had obliged me with a ride for the cost of nearly emptying my coin purse turned back immediately, a curt nod in response to my thanks.

We exchanged an awkward hug.

"Well, I'm alive." I smiled, trying to conceal my shock at his skeletal frame and the squalid condition of the island and lighthouse.

As if reading my thoughts, Papa said, "Lighthouse supply ship was here last week. Told Mr. Wheeler everything'd be repaired and repainted by next spring."

"Mr. Wheeler?" I was surprised.

"Mackelhorn's taken a job at the Lighthouse Board in Detroit."

"Oh." I was relieved at the change while wondering if the new man believed Papa's promises. I doubted Mr. Mackelhorn would have. "I'll help you, Papa."

"Got along just fine alone," he said, going ahead of me up the path to the lighthouse.

I bit my tongue. This was not the time to disagree with him. After settling back into my old room and making an early supper, I asked Papa about the events of the past two years at the lighthouse. He talked about a few rescues he had made and the slight raise in pay he had received. I had steeled myself to answer questions about why I had left and my life in Chicago, but he asked none. I reflected later that night on how little he had changed after all.

While Papa still cleaned and oiled the lamps for our own use and polished the brass and glass of the Fresnel lens now and then, there was no need to keep the lights while the ships were not running. Most of the time he sat in the parlor carving a figure or animal for his newest project, an elaborate nativity scene.

"I must finish every single piece by Christmas," he declared each time he began whittling.

The first months, as fall turned to winter and the lake iced over, I did only the basic chores – making meals, sweeping the floors, and washing clothes. How ironic to be back doing the domestic work I had so gladly shed at Jacob's!

In the evenings, I sat with Papa, reading a few pages in the history books he had gotten since I'd been away while he read and mumbled over the Bible. As early as I could, I went up to my room to secretly draw while sitting on my bed. I longed to show him my drawings, but what if he was still violently opposed to it and went into a rage? Had I traded one prison for another? Oh, I couldn't bear that again, and here I was marooned with Papa through the long winter.

It was awkward not having a table and chair for my work and, after Christmas Day, during which Papa read the Bible and set out the creche scene and we did not exchange gifts, I found myself going up to the tower room at night as soon as I heard Papa snoring. There I could spread out paper on Papa's desk and illuminate my drawing with the light of several lanterns. That first night, I looked through Papa's log before setting it aside for space to draw. I was saddened by his erratic record keeping. In many places, he had skipped the daily entry, and in other places smeared ink made his words illegible. The once firm, clear letters of his handwriting wobbled and wandered the ruled lines. *What had Mr. Wheeler thought when he read it?* I turned back to the day I had arrived. Oct. 12. I remembered a large sailboat passing and saw that Papa had recorded it as a steamship. There was no mention of my return.

I looked around the room. What a place of excitement and fear it had been when I was a child. The night of the fire and lightning striking the ladder as Papa touched it, my frantic lighting of the lantern up in the lens. Being up here again shortly afterwards, terrified to keep the lights while Papa was in town for his mysterious errand. Finding the entry in the log about Dennis Flanagan staying overnight. How could the three of us have known the effect of that fateful toss of the waves on all our lives?

A few weeks later, on the night a blizzard enveloped the island, I was drawing my first picture of Mama and Papa, together in the Tavistock. I chose the moment of Mama rising from her piano bench as Papa in his captain's uniform bowed toward her, the moment of that instant flame of attraction connecting them. Nothing of their unhappiness since then could extinguish that beautiful power, which was still theirs. Scuttling my pencil across the paper in frantic motion, weeping, I sought to capture it all in my drawing. In the noise of the storm and the power of my concentration, I failed to hear the tower door open and Papa come in until he said, "I thought I saw lights up here." I froze in place, silent, as he limped across the room to the desk.

"The log – what are you..." he began. Then he saw what I was doing. With the old thunder in his voice, he barked, "Do I once again have the work of Satan at this lighthouse?"

"Oh, Papa, this has nothing to do with the devil." I heard the tremble in my voice. "See?" I tried to smile. "It's a drawing of you and Mama."

He leaned close and then reeled back as if dealt a blow. "Too real," he muttered.

179

Shivering, I gathered my courage. "Can't you look at it as a gift from God?"

"One that I pray be taken away from you," he said angrily.

"Why, Papa, why?" I cried. "It's what I love to do, was born to do, the only thing I care about."

He pulled himself up straight and glared at me. "Is this why you left?"

I got up and dared to put my arms around him. I barely came to his shoulder. No heat came from him to warm me. "I have to be an artist, a painter, Papa. You forbade it and I had no choice."

He stood still in my embrace for a moment and then moved a hand to pat my hair. "I guess there's no changing what's in the blood," he said, his voice now tired. "My father was determined to be an artist and ruined my mother's life."

"No one knows better than I that doing artist's work does not put food on the table or a roof over your head," I told him.

"How did you do so in Chicago?" he asked.

"With the help of a ...friend – and the piano money."

"Oh, yes, the disappearing piano." A smile creased his face for the first time. "I did wonder what you did with it."

"I sold it to Mr. Mackelhorn," I confessed.

He laughed. "Well, clever girl, good riddance."

"Oh, Papa, I am sorry but I hope whatever ruin I have brought on hurts only myself and not you, or anyone else."

He didn't dispute that but said in an altogether different tone, "I have come to an understanding, Victoria, in my time alone in the lighthouse. That is, God has a plan for each of us, you, Mama, me, even if we don't know what it is."

He ended the conversation there and left me to my work. When I crept down to my bed some hours later, the drawing completed, I wept again and then slept soundly for the first time since my return.

And so the winter dragged on, pulling me with it into a lethargy that rendered me nearly as mute as Papa. Finally, as the ice began to break up and the temperature to rise, I set myself the task, out of desperation, of doing a proper cleaning of the keeper's quarters. Mindlessly, day after day, I scrubbed walls, floors, and windows and wiped chairs and tables with linseed oil. I whitewashed the kitchen walls to cover the soot above the stove and restored the pantry to its proper use, Papa having abandoned his prayers for Mama's return.

In Papa's room, he had maintained the sailor's habit of keeping things orderly but the same layer of grime darkened his bedstead, bureau, floor, and small window, now bare of the curtains Mama had hung there. The clear northerly view of the water gave the illusion of a vast ocean, as if you would have to travel a month to reach land. *Did he sometimes look out and dream he was in his captain's bunk of a morning, checking the sailing weather for the day?*

Finally, I scrubbed my own room. I had turned the dollhouse to the wall the morning I left the lighthouse and it was full of cobwebs and dust, too. I smiled to see the four dolls – Father, Mother, James, and Virginia – still sitting at the kitchen table where I had placed then. I wiped my children's books, turning the pages and smoothing my hand over the pictures. How crude they looked, flat and lifeless scenes, after my years of drawing and painting. My eighth-grade diploma sailed out from the pages of my large fairy tale book, reminding me of my friendless school days save for Mr. Briscoe. I had often thought with dread of my first trip to town in the spring, as much as we needed supplies and I needed a change of scene. I didn't want to see the Fogartys and make up a story about Mama and my life in Chicago. Likewise, Cousin Sherman and Cousin Abigail. But maybe I would visit my old teacher and show him some of my work. The thought cheered me.

March and April were still very cold. Day after day, the winds were wicked, splashing a geyser of waves high up on shore that mesmerized me whenever I looked out. Finally, the weather quieted and the sun shone more days than not. I said, "The keeper's quarters are clean, but we must get Shoreside Light ready for Mr. Wheeler's spring visit, Papa."

"You're right," he said with surprising vigor.

Together, we hauled out the scaffolding, paint, and brushes to whitewash the lighthouse. It took twice as long as it had the last time, owing to Papa's slowness and my reluctance to finish far ahead of him. He had kept the rowboats in decent shape, but the boathouse had several badly rotted boards. We tore them off, nailed new ones in place, and whitewashed the building. I tidied the storage shed and cleaned the chicken

Victoria's Quest

coop, now empty. Papa had sold or killed the chickens in the time I'd been gone. I dug enough weeds out of the garden to plant vegetables.

By the time Mr. Wheeler came ashore in late April, Shoreside Light was a respectable sight. When he finished his work, the inspector said, "Well, Willoughby, you've done quite well."

"My daughter, Victoria, assisted me," Papa said.

"I hope you do not tax your feminine strength," Mr. Wheeler warned, eyeing my short stature and loose hanging work dress.

"I try not to," I said. Papa actually winked at me.

A placard next to the Briscoes' front door invited customers to walk in. Inside, the downstairs parlor was now a reception area with an elegant desk and a small sign, in calligraphy, which said, "Ring Bell for Service. Thank You." Tables on either side of the sofa and chairs displayed sample frames and examples of finished daguerreotypes. I recognized one plump couple as Mr. Briscoe's parents, stiff and unsmiling as were all the other faces and poses. I hoped I had managed to inject more life in my own work. Still, I could see an improvement in photographic techniques, especially sharper images, since I had helped in the studio.

I rang the bell and, after a few moments, the familiar voice floated down. "Trevor?"

I climbed to the third floor with my sketchbook under my arm, calling, "No, Mr. Briscoe. It's an old friend."

He was waiting at the studio doorway, smiling in his imperturbably owlish way. "Why, Victoria! How nice to see you. I heard you were in Chicago. I've been working" – he nodded to the open door of the adjoining darkroom – "so I won't offer you my hand."

"The odor of chemicals I well remember." I smiled.

"I'm sure you do." He looked at me expectantly. "How is your father?"

"I've come back to help him at the lighthouse." Hastily I went on. "And are your parents well?" I realized as I spoke I had heard none of the usual stirrings and voices from their quarters on the second floor.

"Mother and Father have both passed on, alas. They caught a fever, they weren't sure which one was first, but one caught it from the other and they were gone in two weeks."

"Oh, I'm so sorry, Mr. Briscoe."

"I'd be very lonely in this big house if it weren't for my work in the studio."

182

"It looks like you are doing very well in the photography business these days," I said. The studio as I had last seen it held one table of camera supplies, a camera on a tripod, two chairs and a table for customers. Now it was richly appointed with screens, drapery, plants, and other decorative backdrops. The paraphernalia for picture taking filled three tables.

"Yes, I decided to resign from teaching and do this full time." He gestured to one of the chairs. "Please, I'm forgetting my manners. Sit down and tell me what you've been doing in Chicago."

I told him briefly and cryptically that I had taken lessons from an art teacher on drawing portraits and done several private commissions, that I was making progress in skill. "I thought you might like to look at a few of my drawings."

"I would indeed." He took another chair and slowly flipped through the pages. "These are excellent, Victoria. You have much talent."

"You think so?"

"I do," he said solemnly. "I knew you would be successful from the time you sat in my classroom during recess drawing pictures and staring out the window."

"You were kind to me."

Mr. Briscoe blushed, then brightened. "You know, I correspond with some photographers in Chicago. I recall one telling me about an excellent art school. Now what is the name?" He blinked his eyes slowly.

"An art school? I thought they were only out East." *Why had neither Jacob nor Clive ever mentioned it?*

Mr. Briscoe considered. "Perhaps they don't take women. That could be. I'll write my acquaintance and find out more."

"Thank you." I felt a tingle of excitement.

"How long will you stay at the lighthouse?"

"I don't know, but another year at least. My father's health is poor."

Mr. Briscoe's face puckered. "I'm employing an assistant. A young man, Trevor, who works at the printing company. I was expecting him when you called. He will be leaving next spring. Will you think about staying in Shoreside next summer and working for me?"

"What a wonderful idea. I surely would like to, if I can leave my father." After a warm goodbye, I returned to the island with a tiny bit of hope and an equally tiny measure of content.

Entry 24 -- 15 Apr.1868 – Weather: Sunny

Dear Joseph,

    Just a day or two before I give birth, judging by the frequency with which the muscles across my abdomen tighten and relax. Before I struck my bargain with her, Sister Margaret told me to expect them. "You can be thankful there is no pain with these since they are only practice," she said. But each contraction brings a burning pain inside nonetheless. My stomach feels on fire as if from a demon twisting in circles, gleefully jabbing his fork at every tender spot. The torment gets worse when the baby kicks like she wants to force herself through the wall of my stomach instead of arriving the natural way. But Mother Superior says every girl feels the last stage differently. I am afraid of what will happen under Sister Margaret's watch in the birthing room. I recall her checking on Jean, Alice, and Jane once or twice a day when they reached this point, but she does not come near my room. I hope Mother Superior will be alert and protect me. I got a note that Father Gerald wants to meet with me this afternoon...

    I have nearly finished this story. I will use my last strength to write in the log.

Horsewaves
(Summer 1866 - July 1867)

Papa had exerted himself too much in our efforts to ready Shoreside Light for Mr. Wheeler. All summer he had frequent coughing spells and stopped every few steps, gasping for breath, when he climbed the stairs. He got up as early as usual, but dozed most of the day away in his parlor chair. At the end of August, I finally persuaded him to let me maintain the Fresnel lens and wind the winches. I brought down to the kitchen the lanterns for him to clean and fill and the log for him to report the weather and passing ships I observed from the tower window. He also was content for me to make the trips to town for supplies. On my last one before the ships stopped running, I found myself buying a few pieces of canvas, strips of wood to stretch them, and an easel to set up a makeshift studio in the tower room.

One night Papa began a new whittling project, carving a Viking ship. "If I'm doing this, you may as well do that art foolishness right here, too, instead of hiding upstairs," he said gruffly. Happily, I moved everything down from the tower and set it up in the space where Mama's piano had stood.

"Oh, Papa, please let me do your portrait," I begged.

He looked up from his work, closed his eyes, shook his head, then opened his eyes again. "If you must, you must," he said, breathing a deep sigh that set off a coughing fit.

"Just continue whittling, Papa," I said, already beginning to sketch him, tensed with his knife over a piece of wood. In my portrait, I restored the health he had lost, giving him a ruddy complexion, firm cheeks, and muscled arms. My hand seemed to wield the brush without conscious effort in giving life to his image on the canvas. Papa surprised me with his patience. Every night he dutifully struck the same whittling pose and, as I painted, talked to me of his early days on the sea. A few weeks later, when I told him the portrait was done and turned the easel for him to see, he once again surprised, no, shocked me by laughing, an occurrence so rare I could not remember the last time I had heard it.

"Is that my long lost twin you've painted there, Victoria? I haven't looked in a mirror for years but I know I don't look that good or that young. But thank you," he said, and in his words I heard affection, if not love, and was filled with joy.

In the waning weeks of winter, an idea had seized me, both waking and dreaming, that I must paint seascapes outdoors when the weather warmed. What exactly I would paint I didn't know yet, only that I must, and on my first trip to Shoreside in April I carried back to the island an entire roll of wide canvas for the project.

Immediately, I began a fevered study of the blues of the water and the variety of waves produced by the constantly changing force and direction of wind. Mornings, afternoons, evenings as long as there was light to see, I would sit on a rock or walk along the shore observing colors and motion. Most often the lake appeared its usual grayish blue or green, even brown, but sometimes the light created a hue of teal or even violet. Later, I'd spend hours in the parlor mixing squibs of blue, white, yellow, red, and black, dabbing the most successful replicas of colors on a spare square of canvas.

One blustery, bright morning at the end of April, I stood by the boathouse watching a wave roll toward the lighthouse from far out, cresting high, spitting out foam. It was then, as I stared in a hypnotic gaze, I saw my first horse, the head of Paul's adored Sandy, tossing in the darkness of the curling wave. I squinted against the sun. *Was it a momentary mirage, a trick of the eye, a confusion of my mind?* The wave crashed into the island, and Sandy disappeared. I looked out again where another wave galloped toward me, and there was the straining neck of the farmer's black runaway I had tried to draw. I stood there, riveted by my vision of other horses of my past, the massive firehouse horse, the head-hanging old work horse, the high-stepping carriage horse, the restless stable horse, the proud Army horse. If not a whole horse, some part appeared in every wave, no matter the size – a mane, a hoof, a tail, ears, a nose – each shake of the water like a kaleidoscope that made a magical new horse pattern.

That night the ghost returned in a robe soaked with lake water. In my sleep, waves roared in my ears and when I started awake, my face was wet. Now I knew what I was to paint: A glorious, mysterious mingling of waves and horses.

Early the next morning, as the sun warmed me and breezes danced around me, I pounded together a large frame and stretched canvas over it. It was too large to fit my easel, so I propped it against the flagpole, the red and white cloth waving like a scarf as if to call attention to me. Palette in

187

hand, I looked out trustingly on the water, and there was Sandy again, her golden flanks reflected by the sun, her white mane flying in a long, bubbling wave. The image imprinted like a photograph in my mind's eye as I used to fix a street scene in Chicago, and I set to work without a further glance at the lake. Never had I felt such joy in painting, my brush moved with wild, bold strokes across the canvas to capture my vision. How glorious it was to paint in the open air, safe and free! I had no notion of time, of being thirsty or hungry, of my legs aching from standing or my arms from lifting. As shadows fell across the grass, Papa appeared at my side.

"Good heavens, girl, what are you doing?" He gaped at the mass of streaked lines and curves, the chaos of colors and shapes that to me were all Sandys, the one who cantered on the beach, the one who pushed her eager head over the fence for a pat, the one who nibbled on an apple from Paul's hand.

"Can't you see them, Papa? Horses in the waves?"

"Horses!" he exclaimed. "A very strange notion of Lake Michigan is all I see."

I thought then I might be mad to see what Papa did not, but your voice, Joseph, came to me suddenly. "You must not give up your art," and I was soothed – this was exactly what I was meant to paint.

The whole month of May, I worked on that canvas and two others. Embedded in the waves of the second were handsome, dark horses pulling carriages at a dignified, confident trot and in the stormy third and final one, panicked horses bolting from fire or whips or cracks of lightning. After my first rendering of each canvas, I carried it inside to the parlor. Each morning I would look at all three and decide there was something wrong with the shapes, colors, or composition of one or another.

Papa, watching, would groan, "Not again," as I carried one out for another day's work. The task seemed as unceasing as the waves, but I could not stop until I was satisfied, even if no one other than Papa ever saw them, and if no one at all ever saw in the paintings my vision of horses.

One overcast, foggy morning in June, I peered from the tower and thought I saw a capsized boat east of the island. I went downstairs and told Papa I would take a rowboat out to investigate. He was heating the kettle to make himself a pot of tea. "Cold," he said, and I thought it was my haste that made me feel so contrarily warm. I grew hotter rowing out to the boat, which turned out to be only a wide swath of dark seaweed. I drifted a while, cooling off, and it was an hour before I returned to the island. Coming up the path, I saw with alarm the lighthouse door standing open. I ran inside to find the air smelling charred and Papa crumpled on the kitchen floor next to an overturned bucket of water. The kettle on the stove must have boiled dry and started a fire he tried to put out.

"Oh, no, Papa!" I cried. I flung myself down next to him and picked up one rough hand. It was ice cold. "Papa!" His eyes were open, staring at the ceiling. I put a trembling hand on his chest and bent down to put my ear close to his nose and mouth. Not a stir of breath. I put my arms around him, feeling my own chest tight and drained of oxygen. I stayed there a long time, holding him, feeling that I was floating somewhere above the two of us, until finally tears came and I began to sob.

The next morning, after a sleepless night in the tower, I rowed to town for help. Michael Willoughby and two men from Willie's followed me in a large boat. Michael had grown stout like his father and adopted his pompous way of talking. "Father will make arrangements for Cousin Edward's burial in our family plot and for someone to come out to keep the lights until a new keeper can be appointed. Cousin Edward was always so proud. Wouldn't take help no matter what Father said. Can you manage one more day alone?" he said all in one speech.

"Yes, thank you." I went to Papa's room, which I had not entered for weeks, for his captain's uniform that I knew he would want to be buried in. On the bureau was an envelope with my name in Papa's wobbly scrawl. Inside were ten twenty-dollar bills.

Papa was buried with a simple graveside service conducted by the Lutheran minister and attended only by Cousin Sherman, Michael, and me. Cousin Abigail, it was explained, could not bear to come to the cemetery where her son was buried. I was sure she also had no wish to see me. Nor had the Fogartys. At my request, someone from Willie's had delivered the news to them of Papa's death, but there had been no response, either from anger or hurt. I didn't blame them for thinking me indifferent to old ties of friendship rather than the truth, that I did not know how to tell them about what had happened to Mama and to me.

Afterwards, Cousin Sherman took me to the lunch at the Tavistock, which now had a separate dining area that welcomed ladies.

"I'll miss your father. He was a good man. Stubborn but good."

"Yes," I agreed. "I hope you know we've been grateful to you. Arranging for me to go to school in town and getting Papa the keeper post."

"I did my best," he said, winking and waving his cigar. There was a bit of the old Cousin Sherman left, I was glad to see.

"What will you do now?" he asked, exhaling a stream of smoke that stung my eyes.

"Go back to Chicago. Papa left me a little money."

Cousin Sherman pulled out his wallet and handed me several bills without looking at them. "Well, here's a bit more. Wondered why you didn't ask me before. I was always fond of you. No one else needed to know," he added, and I knew he meant Cousin Abigail.

He mentioned death only once more in the course of our meal – not Papa's or Paul's, but President Lincoln's when his funeral train passed through Shoreside to the great thrill of the townspeople.

A few weeks later, I left the island to the care of a new keeper, a man who had worked at Willie's. I had the information from Mr. Briscoe that, yes, The Chicago School of Painting accepted women. My old mentor also agreed to store Papa's and Sadie's portrait and the three large paintings, which I had titled Horsewaves. The change in my fortunes, returning to Chicago to go to painting school, to once again live as an artist: There seemed to be no more reality to what was happening than there had been to my visions on canvas.

Entry 25 — 17 Apr.1868 — Weather: Raging wind

Dear Joseph,

I addressed this log to you from the beginning, imagining you reading it, sighing and nodding and smiling through my accounts, though knowing you could never do so. I do hope our daughter reads it someday, perhaps looking at my drawing of you and wearing the bracelet – I must believe that. Elise found me writing this final entry amid such piercing pain that she has gone to find Sister Margaret...

Joseph
(Chicago, August 1867 - February 1868)

I rented a small room near The Chicago School of Painting. How eagerly I climbed the stairs that first late August morning in the old building on Michigan Avenue to the large room with white painted walls and windows that looked out to the lake. How unhappily I discovered I was the only female and Mr. Eliot, the mop-haired instructor with fiery eyes, would have only cutting words for my efforts that day and every day thereafter.

The first Saturday, discouraged, I went to see my only friends left in Chicago, the Wingates, and found you, Joseph, packing for a month's journey to the South to escort another group of Negroes up to Canada. With a cheerful grin, you said you had managed to stir Sadie and George into action, and they were already in Canada helping with the effort. We sat and talked all day, you of your mission and I of my art, and fate, and there was a moment when we ceased speaking and held hands and I thought how beautiful and right the colors of our skins side by side. We reached for each other at the same moment. We knew so little of each other and yet it seemed we knew everything we needed to. Perhaps we have been together in some other time and world that we were permitted to know in this lifetime only through the creation of a new life. I had thought I could not conceive a child, having not done so either by Paul or Jacob. Fate, my dearest Joseph. For that one day of our lovemaking, I was fertile.

When I returned a month later, I was grief-stricken to learn from a neighbor that you had been killed by a rabid white plantation owner in Georgia. A month after that, broken-hearted, I knew I was going to have a child. Miserable, ill, frightened, I could tell no one of my condition. As fall turned to winter, I covered myself in thick coats and vomited every morning and evening, dragging myself in between to school classes. The results on my easel worsened every week until one feverish day I remembered St. Mary's Haven.

So, now I am saved by means I am not proud of but could not help. Sadie and George should be home now to take our baby. I will go with Elise to Philadelphia and once again take up the artist's life. I have done all I can for now.

Oh, here is Sister Margaret at my door...

Epilogue

Victoria Willoughby died on April 19, 1868, at 6 a.m. shortly after giving birth to an infant girl. Her labor was long and hard, and she was found to have an abnormally narrow pelvis and a severe internal infection. While she was conscious, though she could not speak, Father Gerald administered the last rites of the Catholic Church and baptized the infant. Victoria was first buried in Lincoln Park Cemetery. Her remains were later moved at the request of Sherman Willoughby to the family plot in Shoreside, Indiana.

Victoria's daughter was named Margaret and raised by Sadie and George Wingate of Chicago. Margaret married Wilmer Jefferson, like herself a mulatto, as the child of a Negro and of a white parent was called then. She bore a daughter, Kathleen, in 1887 and spent her life improving the conditions of housing in her neighborhood. She was fond of boat rides on the lake but died, ironically, when a horse trampled her in the street.

Kathleen was light and married a white man. They formed a vaudeville team to entertain in music halls of the early 1900s. She later marched for women's suffrage and spent six months in jail for that cause. She was said to have a heart of gold and died when that heart gave out, leaving little more than a trunk of glittery costumes and a voter's card.

Her daughter, Anna, was born in 1913. She trained to be a nurse and joined the Navy to go overseas as a nurse during World War II. In Italy, she met and married a refugee, nearly dying in the course of giving birth to their daughter, Jane, in 1943. Back in the United States, she volunteered for Margaret Sanger's birth control campaign. Later, she developed mental problems and died in an automobile accident.

Jane grew up loving to ride horses and was the first generation to go to college. On her first job after graduation, she met and married an ambitious business executive. Against his wishes, she became a Vietnam peace activist soon after the birth of her daughter, Victoria, in 1968. She used her divorce settlement to open a non-profit agency serving homeless people. She died of a sudden heart attack.

Victoria Cameron is a photographer and the single mother of a daughter named Vanessa. She has not disclosed the father's identity. She has possession of Victoria's diary, which has been passed on through the women of the family, and a single existing photograph of her in a daguerreotype of the Sherman Willoughby family. Victoria's bracelet and drawing of Joseph disappeared somewhere in the first few generations. From time to time, she takes her camera to the beach on windy days. There, she peers through the lens across the lake at the abandoned lighthouse, and, as the waves whip toward her, kicking foam, tries to capture on film the watery shapes of wild horses.

The Works of Victoria Willoughby

Horsewaves Series (1867), Indiana State Art Museum, courtesy of the estate of Henry Briscoe (also exhibited in the Women's Pavilion of the Columbian Exposition of 1893 in Chicago, sponsored by Miss Elise Farnsworth's Photography Studio of Philadelphia).

Portrait of Edward Willoughby (1867), *Portrait of Sadie Wingate* (1866), Shoreside Historical Society, courtesy of the estate of Michael Willoughby.

Sketches and Still Lives of St. Mary's Haven (1868), The Chicago School of Painting, donated by Sister Vincent Marie, Mother Superior of St. Mary's Haven.

About the Author

Nancy Hagen Patchen has a B.A. in English from the University of Michigan. For many years, she was a newspaper reporter and editor. Her short stories have appeared in several anthologies including *Prairie Hearts: Women View the Midwest; Alternatives: Roads Less Travelled;* and *Mystery Time.* Her creative nonfiction has been published in *The Little Red Writing Book – A Practical Guide to Writing Your Own Life Story* and *The Reality of Breastfeeding – Reflections by Contemporary Women.* She lives in West Lafayette, Indiana.

To Order Additional Copies...

Just send check or money order for $15.95 for each copy of *Victoria's Quest* ordered plus shipping and handling as follows:

For one copy ....Add $3.95
For Two ....Add $5.95
For Each Additional Book ....Add $1.65

Indiana residents: add $1 sales tax for each copy ordered.

Make payable to

Writer Works
1133 Glenway Street
West Lafayette, IN 47906

Questions?
Email us at writerworks@verizon.net

200